Positive
Deception

D1121351

Positive Deception

LaCricia A`ngelle

Newbern, Tennessee

This is a work of fiction. The characters, incidents, and dialogues are products of the author's imagination and are not to be construed as real. Any references to actual events, persons, living or dead, or to real locales are intended to give the novel a sense of reality.

Positive Deception
Published by His Pen Publishing, LLC
Newbern, Tennessee 38059

ISBN-10: 0-9798020-3-2
ISBN-13: 978-0-9798020-3-4

Library of Congress Control Number: 2012915313

First Printing August 2012
Printed in the United States of America

10 9 8 7 6 5 4 3 2 1

Bible Scriptures taken from New King James Version and New International Version

This book is also available in digital ebook format

This book is dedicated to
All those that have faced
difficult situations and felt like
no one cares or understands.
God cares, He loves you and He
is concerned about you.
You are never alone.

Acknowledgments

First and foremost, I give thanks to my Heavenly Father for entrusting me with such a precious gift. This book would not have been possible without Him. Thank you, Lord for your patience with me.

To my beloved husband, Christopher. Your love and support has encouraged me through the roughest part of this project.

To my loving children, Keshonna, Larry, Ayonna, Gabrielle, and Samantha. I thank God for you all. Thank you for your patience with me while I worked on this book. I love you all more than words could ever express.

To my parents Murry, and Emma, and my daddy Felix (in heaven above.) Thank you for shaping me into the woman that I am. Thank you, Mama for encouraging me and helping me to give birth to the ministry that God has placed within me.

To my sisters, nieces, and nephews, and my loving in-laws. I love you all. Thank you for loving me.

To my best friend, Author, Shelia E. Lipsey. I can't thank you enough for all your hard work, and dedication, and most importantly for keeping me on track. Thank you forever and always.

Special thanks to Dr. Monique Casey-Bolden for helping me to keep my facts straight, and Ms. January at the United Center in Chicago for answering all my questions.

Finally to Readers, and Book clubs everywhere. Thank you for taking time out to read this book. I pray it is a blessing to you.

Be Blessed,
LaCricia A`ngelle

Other Books by LaCricia A`ngelle

Girl, Naw!

Available in Print and Digital format
at online retailers and bookstores

Prologue

"Good morning, Miss. Please come with me," the nurse directed. With a manila folder in her hand, she turned and smiled at the young woman. Unable to decipher if the smile was one of pity or genuine, the young woman followed close behind. The hallway felt cold and impersonal. The nurse stopped at a room that housed a large oak desk with a tall, black leather chair nestled behind it. Stacks of folders lay disheveled on the desk next to a flat screen computer monitor and wireless keyboard.

Pointing to the chairs in front of the desk, the nurse encouraged the young lady to have a seat. "The doctor will be with you in just a moment. Please, make yourself comfortable."

The young lady sat still, barely breathing. Beads of sweat formed on her nose. With a single motion, she wiped her nose with the back of her hand. Her mind raced. What if the doctor gave her news she didn't want. What would she do then? This could change her life forever. All of her plans and dreams would be altered. Reaching into her bag, she pulled out a bottle of water, opened it, and took a sip.

"Sorry for the delay, I was tied up with another patient," the doctor explained as he walked into the room. He gently shook her hand before taking a seat behind his desk. Opening the file folder, he carefully reviewed her test results. Inhaling deeply, he rubbed his chin vigorously.

Looking up at the young lady, he could tell by the expression on her face that she was nervous. With a firm tone he said, "I've reviewed your test results, and I'm sorry to say the results are positive." The doctor looked at the fragile young woman that sat before him. This was the news he hated to share with a patient. Reaching into his desk drawer, he pulled out several pamphlets and handed them to her.

The young lady sat motionless and remained silent. Instantly, her heart dropped. Her life would never be the same.

Chapter 1

One day that space is going to be mine. Maxwell Lee peered at the sign marked 'PASTOR' as he drove through the church parking lot searching for an available space. After pulling his Cadillac Escalade into the vacant spot next to Deacon Murray's car, he flipped down the sun visor and checked his teeth to make sure his smile was perfect. The last thing he needed was an unsightly pepper left over from his breakfast burrito cramping his style. Popping his collar, Maxwell smiled broadly, "Perfect as usual." Reaching over to the passenger side, he picked up his Bible case and hurried into the church.

Sister Charlotte Day welcomed Maxwell with a motherly embrace. "Good morning, Minister Lee," she said. "Are you blessed of the Lord this morning?"

"Blessed and highly favored, Sister Day," he replied enthusiastically.

"That's what I'm talkin' about. Give God the glory, son."

Maxwell had become accustomed to Sister Day's "attitude check" as she gleefully referred to her usual greeting. When he first began attending Christ the True Vine Church, he wasn't sure how to respond to Sister Day. He thought her greeting meant he needed a password in order to enter the church. Thankfully, Deacon Murray who was following close behind him sensed his confusion and blurted out an exuberant "Yes,

Lord," pulling Charlotte's attention away from him.

"Good morning, Minister." Pastor James's bass voice cut into his reflections, drawing Maxwell's attention back to the present.

"Good morning, Pastor James, Sister James. How are you all doing this morning?"

"Doing fine, Minister. We're doing just fine. The Good Lord has blessed me to open my eyes to see yet another day that wasn't promised to me. He allowed me to look into the eyes of my beautiful wife once again. Yes, sir, I am doing fine."

Sister James tried to mask her blushing. After fifty years of marriage, he still had that effect on her. Pulling gently on her husband's arm, she smiled at Maxwell and quickly disappeared into the congregation.

Parishioners filed into the church sanctuary, preparing for the start of service. Maxwell made his way to the platform and took his usual seat adjacent to Pastor James.

Standing to their feet in unison, like a well-trained army, the choir led the congregation in a high tempo praise song. Maxwell nodded his head as he rocked from side to side with the beat of the music.

Once the choir concluded their selection, Maxwell approached the podium. He looked out over the congregation and studied the faces of the many parishioners in attendance. Within five years, he had watched the congregation grow from a faithful fifty members to well over four hundred.

Clearing his throat, Maxwell led the congregation in prayer. Making every effort to pray hard, he prayed as if he was preaching a sermon. When he finished, he noticed he had several admirers in the congregation. Being a single minister, he had gotten used to all of the extra attention. There was always some woman approaching him, giving him her phone number, and

requesting *special* prayer. He had dated a fev
church, but made no commitments. Maxwel
was a desperate woman. In many ways, he
and still enjoyed the thrill of the chase.

Returning to his seat, he settled in and offered his support to the rest of the service. The choir, consisting of mostly teenagers and young adults, belted out more songs of praise. Members of the congregation stood to their feet as they clapped and swayed to the music.

Pastor James rose to the podium and delivered a dynamic message. His voice trembled, revealing his maturity.

That should be me up there preaching. I should be the Pastor, Maxwell thought. During the five years since he became a member of Christ the True Vine, he had seen a number of positive changes take place. When he first started attending the church, he had come at the invitation of Pastor James. Pastor James had been a frequent shopper in Maxwell's clothing store, and after several invites, Maxwell finally accepted the pastor's invitation and made his arrival. Prior to attending Christ the True Vine, Maxwell hadn't attended church in over a year. He used the success of his business as an excuse not to attend. When he received church invitations, he normally responded by saying he had to work on Sundays. There was something about the atmosphere at Christ the True Vine that made it feel like home to him. The members of the congregation treated him with kindness and concern. Several people approached him, making him feel welcome. He became a member the same day and had been faithful ever since.

The church didn't have many children or young adults when he first started attending. There were a few that came with their parents, but overall, the congregation was made up of people age forty and above. Maxwell worked closely with Pastor James ιelp increase church membership. He suggested having a ɪent revival in Ogden Park as a way to attract people. Pastor James agreed, and after obtaining the proper permits, Maxwell started promoting the revival. He handed out flyers at his store, throughout the mall, and the surrounding neighborhood. He sent letters to various churches and community choirs requesting their attendance. The response was overwhelming. Numerous people showed up for the event. Although some of them were drawn by the music, Pastor James's message of Jesus' love and a better way of life compelled many to begin attending the church after the close of the revival. The increase in church membership brought a diverse group of individuals, including a large number of children, teens, and young adults. Maxwell played a big part in developing activities geared towards the younger members.

****

Following the conclusion of Pastor James's message, and dismissal of service, Maxwell mingled among the crowd, greeting church members and introducing himself to visitors. He noticed a beautiful young woman he hadn't seen at the church before who looked to be about twenty-five years old, gathering her belongings at the back of the church. He knew she was a visitor, but he didn't get to see if she had come with someone, or if she had come alone. As he began walking in the woman's direction, Sister Hazel Sherrill stepped in front of him.

"How are you today, Minister Lee?" she asked, smiling broadly.

Maxwell extended his hand and replied, "I'm doing well, Sister Sherrill. How are you?"

He tried to be cordial, but Sister Sherrill was working his

last nerve, blabbing on and on about what he felt was crazy stuff. He didn't care that on her way to church some man with Florida license plates had cut her off on the Dan Ryan Expressway. He wanted to get to the back of the church to see who the beautiful woman was. Maxwell nodded his head in agreement as Sister Sherrill spoke, hoping she would hurry up. Looking over Hazel's head, he noticed the woman walking out the door.

"I did good, Minister Lee. I didn't curse that man out or flip him off. I know I'm growing in the Lord because I remember the time when I would have let him have it," Sister Sherrill proudly stated.

She had barely finished her sentence before Maxwell cut in. "Wow, Sis Sherrill, you're right. It is a blessing you were able to stay saved by resisting the urge to curse that man out. I agree with you, that does show you are really growing in your relationship with the Lord. Praise, God."

Shaking her hand vigorously, Maxwell smiled and said, "Now if you will excuse me, I need to speak to a few other people before they leave. God bless you, sister."

Hazel stood looking at Maxwell like he had lost his mind. He had never rushed her off like that before. On top of that, he kept looking away while she spoke to him. She looked around hoping to find out who was distracting him, but found no one.

Maxwell stepped out of the door, only to discover the woman was gone. Rubbing his hand over the top of his low cut, wavy, black hair, he stood astonished. Disappointed, he returned inside the church, grabbed his Bible case, and headed home.

Reaching into his jacket pocket, he pulled out his cell phone and turned it on. The display screen indicated he had three voicemail messages. He pressed the button to retrieve his messages.

"Hey, baby. It's your mama. Give me a call when you get out of church."

The second message was a clicking sound indicating the caller had hung up without leaving a message.

Why do people bother to listen to the entire greeting and then hang up? Pressing the button, he deleted the message. The next message was from his brother, Jason.

"Hey, bruh. Man, look, give me a call when you get a chance. You will never believe who I ran into today. Call me. A'ight. Holla."

Jason had piqued his curiosity, but right now, he needed to get home, change clothes, and get ready for the Bulls game. A short drive later, Maxwell arrived at his townhouse and made his way upstairs. Just as he entered his bedroom, his home telephone rang. Removing the cordless phone from its base, he pressed the Talk button.

"Hello."

"Boy, did you get my message? I told you to call me when you got out of church."

"Hey, Ma. How you doing?" Maxwell replied calmly.

"I'm doing all right. How was church today?"

Maxwell loosened his tie, and removed his jacket. "God moved in a great way."

"That's good, baby," Marilyn replied, relaxing her tone.

"So, what's going on, Ma? You sounded a little upset when I answered the phone."

"Nothing too much. I'm a bit tired, that's all," she replied. "Jason was over here earlier. He said he had been trying to get in touch with you."

"Yeah, I got his message. I'm going to call him in a few."

"Okay, I just wanted to make sure you were doing all right. You ain't called your mama in a while."

Here comes the guilt trip, he thought.

"You don't ever get too grown for your mama," she continued, slowly dragging her words as she spoke.

"I know, Ma. I haven't forgotten about you. I'll come by there Wednesday after work."

"All right. In that case, I'll fix you some dinner."

"That sounds good, Ma. I'll see you then." Maxwell pressed the End button, tossed the phone onto the bed, and finished changing his clothes.

After putting on lounge pants and a t-shirt, he went into the kitchen and heated up some leftover baked chicken. Maxwell sat down in front of the television, and put his plate on the coffee table. Jamming a forkful of fries into his mouth, he switched on the television with the remote control, and flipped through the channels.

The telephone rang loudly, commanding his attention. Glancing at the caller ID, Maxwell recognized Jason's number on the display and picked up.

"What up, what up, what up?" Maxwell bellowed.

"Man, what's up, dawg? You can't call nobody back?" Jason replied irritably.

"Naw, man. It ain't like that. I just got home a little while ago. I hadn't had a chance to call you yet. What's going on?"

"You won't believe who I ran into this morning."

Maxwell sat up straight on the couch. Jason had his full attention. "Who?"

"Maxine Miller."

Excited, Maxwell asked, "Are you talking about the girl we used to call M&Ms from the East Side? Man, that was my girl."

"Yeah," Jason teased. "I thought you would remember her. Man, that girl practically had you doing back flips. You were crazy about her."

Maxwell smiled at the reflection. "Where did you see her? How's she doing? Is she married? She got any kids?"

"Slow up, dawg." Jason laughed. "One question at a time. I ran into her at Walgreens over on sixty- second and Western. She said she's doing good. Got a nice little gig, too. I think she said she's a tax or real estate attorney, or something like that. Ole' girl look good."

"For real," Maxwell nodded his head while listening to Jason.

"She asked about you. I told her you were doing the church thing now. Mane, she got excited when I told her that. She said she's into church too. She gave me her number and told me to have you to call her."

Alright. I'll get it from you later. The Bulls game is about to start."

"Okay, man. Holla at me later."

Maxwell ended his call with Jason and returned the phone to its base. It had been years since he had seen Maxine. They were friends throughout elementary school, but had lost touch when her family moved out of town. He would give her a call, but it was going to have to wait until after the game.

Chapter 2

"Where are my keys?" Lina yelled, flipping over the couch cushions. "This always happens when I'm running late." Rays of sunlight beamed through the window, casting a reflection on a small, metal object on the coffee table. "There they are," she mouthed. "Finally, I'm good to go."

Lina took one final look in the mirror. This would be her first time attending church with her friend, Cheri, and she didn't want to arrive late. Within seconds, she bolted out the door. Jumping into her midnight blue Chevy Cobalt, she carefully pulled out of the apartment complex parking lot and headed south on Halsted to Marquette Road. Turning right, she continued west until she reached Loomis Street. Lina tapped her fingers on the steering wheel to the beat of the music while she waited for the light to turn green before making a left turn. Within seconds, she arrived in front of the large brick building. The sign out front displayed the words Christ the True Vine Church. "I hope I'm not late," she muttered. She spotted an empty space marked Visitor, parked her car, then got out and headed for the door.

Cheri was standing outside the entrance, waiting for her when she arrived. "Girl, hurry up. Service is about to start." She gave Lina a quick hug and escorted her into the sanctuary.

Cheri pointed out two seats near the back. Since it was Lina's first time at Christ the True Vine, Cheri thought she would feel more comfortable sitting closer to the rear of the church. They quietly took their seats before the choir started singing.

Lina sat attentively, taking in every phase of the service. She was impressed by the choir. Before she knew it, she was on her feet clapping and singing along. She smiled, as memories of her days as the choir director at her home church in Durham flooded her mind. If she had not been looking directly at them, she would never have guessed they were a youth choir.

Struggling to remain focused during the prayer, Lina wondered if the young minister was praying or delivering a short sermon. She resisted the urge to look up to see if he was dancing around the podium. When Pastor James got up and delivered the message, she was pulled into his powerful sermon about the tests and triumph of Job.

After the closing prayer, Lina gathered her belongings and quietly headed toward the door. Cheri followed close behind, greeting fellow congregants as she passed.

"How did you like the service?" Cheri asked, once she and Lina were outside.

"I enjoyed it. I'll definitely come back again. Your pastor is a powerful speaker." Opening her car door, Lina tossed her Bible and purse inside.

"Girl, you had them brothers breaking their necks trying to look at you in that sassy yellow dress."

"I didn't even notice." Crossing her arms, Lina stated firmly, "That's not what I came for. The last thing I need right now is a man bringing me drama. That is one road in my life that is closed for repairs."

Cheri looked at her friend with compassion and understanding. Although she didn't know the full details of what Lina had endured at the hands of her ex-boyfriend, she knew it was enough to justify Lina's current attitude towards men.

"So. girl, what are you about to do?"

Lina smiled at her friend, "Nothing too much, go home, get out of this dress, and throw these shoes as far back in the closet as I can possibly get them. My feet are killing me."

Cheri laughed at the look of agony on Lina's face. "Girl, I've told you about wearing those 'cute' shoes; they will tear your feet up."

Lina laughed. "I know. I thought they were three-hour shoes, but I found out they expired after thirty minutes. My dogs are barking."

The friends shared another laugh and a hug before parting ways. Lina agreed to call Cheri once she made it home.

****

Lina walked through the door of her small, one bedroom apartment, and immediately kicked off her shoes. "Whew, relief," she bellowed, pressing her feet into the thick, plush carpet. She slowly walked into her bedroom and changed her clothes. She didn't realize how tired she was. Surrendering to her body's demands, she laid across the bed for a short nap.

"Living my life like its golden, living my life like its golden." Lina jumped up from the bed and reached for her cell phone. Pressing the green button, she answered groggily, "Hello."

"I'm glad I wasn't holding my breath waiting on you to call me, because I would be dead as a door knob by now."

"Cheri, girl you're crazy. I fell asleep as soon as I got home. I didn't realize I was that tired."

"I know how that is. I'll just talk to you later."

"No, you're good," Lina replied groggily.

"I'm glad you came to church today."

"Me too. I've visited several churches in the two years that I've been in Chicago, but your church reminds me the most of my home church in Durham. I'm glad you invited me."

"That's what I'm here for. Lord knows someone has to keep you straight."

Chapter 3

"Max...Max...Maxwell." Simon stood in front of Maxwell's desk holding a box full of shirts.

Puzzled, Maxwell looked up at Simon. "What's up, man? Why are you calling me like that?"

Sitting the box down, Simon replied, "You mean, what's up with you? I've been standing here calling you for a while. Where's your head?"

Rubbing his hand across his face, Maxwell exhaled roughly. "I have a lot on my mind. What do you need?"

There was no way Maxwell was going to tell Simon he had spent all morning thinking about the mystery woman he saw at church. Not only was she beautiful, but when she joined in on the praise and worship, she stood out even more. Her attentiveness to the service, and apparent love for the Lord made her more attractive.

Simon had worked with Maxwell long enough to know not to press him to talk. It was best to drop the subject. Maxwell kept most of his thoughts private.

"I need you to check the box of shirts that just arrived. They're the ones you special ordered from New York."

Maxwell pointed to a cabinet behind his desk. "Put them back there. I'll check them in a minute."

Simon placed the box on the cabinet and left the office.

Massaging his temples, Maxwell inhaled deeply, then slowly exhaled. Picking up his now warm Pepsi, he swallowed the remnants and stood up from his desk. "Back to work," he murmured, pulling the stack of shirts from the box. Maxwell carefully inspected each garment before carrying them to the sales floor.

Following a quick steam press, he grabbed a box containing wooden hangers and carefully placed each new shirt on the sales rack.

*****

Lina pressed the talk button on her wireless headset, hoping to catch the incoming call before it transferred to voicemail.

"Lina Fairweather speaking, how can I help you?"

"Whatever, girl. Don't be trying to sound all dignified with me. I know the real you," Cheri joked, as she repeated Lina's greeting with mock sarcasm.

"Girl, had I known it was you I wouldn't have wasted my breath. I would have simply answered with, what is it, problem child. What do you want, with your crazy self?"

The friends shared a laugh.

"Whatcha doing?" Cheri asked playfully.

"I'm on my way to The Plaza. My father's birthday is next week, and I need to get him a gift. I hope I can find him something at one of the men's shops there. Daddy is so hard to shop for. He's old fashioned, and he never wants me to spend any money on him. I'm going to surprise him this time by sending his gift through FedEx, so he can't reject it."

"Dang. It's been a while since I've been to The Plaza. The last time I was there, one of my favorite authors had a book signing at that Christian bookstore."

Lina crossed the intersection and made a right turn into the large parking lot. Driving slowly, she scanned the parking lot for an open spot. "What are you up to?" she asked.

"Nothing. Lying here watching TV. Why don't you call

me when you finish. Maybe we can catch a movie or go get something to eat."

"Okay, that sounds good. I'll call you in a little while." Lina pulled her small car into an empty parking spot and turned off the ignition. Grabbing her purse, she locked her car and dashed into the crowded mall. Once inside, Lina maneuvered her way through the crowd of shoppers browsing each of the men's stores. She stopped briefly at Victoria's Secret to replenish her stock of fragrant lotions and soaps. Once she was satisfied with her selection, she resumed her search for her father's gift. Taking the escalator to the lower level, Lina noticed a mannequin in the window of a men's store wearing an ivory colored, silk shirt. *Daddy would love that,* she thought, and swiftly walked into the store.

Maxwell walked through the store straightening racks of clothes and greeting customers. He blinked rapidly like he was trying to make sure his eyes weren't playing tricks on him. He couldn't believe it, but standing less than 100 feet away from him was the woman he couldn't stop thinking about. The one he desperately wanted to meet at church.

"Is there something I can help you with, Miss?" he asked as he approached her.

Lina looked up from the mannequin, acknowledging the sales clerk. "Actually, I could use some help. I want this shirt in a size seventeen and a thirty-six/thirty-seven sleeve length. It's for a tall man. I also want the best tie set and cuff links you have."

Maxwell was taken aback. Lina appeared to be very direct. He was going to have to calculate his moves carefully. Smiling, he said, "A woman who knows exactly what she wants. Impressive. A lot of ministers buy this shirt."

Lina frowned. Peering at him directly she asked, "And

that's relevant because?"

Unable to hide his embarrassment, Maxwell smiled and replied, "You look like a minister's wife." Placing his hand on his chest he continued, "Now if you'll excuse me, I'll pull my foot out my mouth."

Lina returned his smile. "A minister's wife, huh. That's the first time I've been told that. It's very surprising, especially coming from a salesman." Staring curiously at Maxwell, she stated, "You look familiar. Have I seen you before?"

Maxwell was ecstatic. There he was trying to figure out how to reveal his identity, and instead she did it for him. "Last Sunday, you visited the church I attend, Christ the True Vine."

"Oh, I remember now. You're the minister that did the opening prayer," she said with a smirk.

"You remember my prayer? I'm impressed."

"How could I forget? I spent most of the prayer trying to figure out if you were praying or if you were preaching."

"Oh, you got jokes. That's okay. I can appreciate a woman with a sense of humor."

Lina rolled her eyes and smiled. "Who's joking? I'm serious."

Maxwell extended his hand toward Lina. "Since I've made such an odd first impression the only thing left to do is formally introduce myself. I'm Maxwell Lee."

Confused, Lina shook his hand and repeated, "Maxwell? Isn't that the name of this store?"

"Yes, it is. I'm the owner."

"Oh, okay. In that case, Mr. Lee, would you kindly show me the tie sets and cuff links."

"Of course, right this way." Maxwell grabbed the shirt Lina selected from the rack and escorted her to the requested items.

Lina followed close behind as Maxwell directed her to a glass display case in the center of the store. She carefully studied the various sets of tie pins and cuff links before selecting a gold set with a diamond stud in the middle. Next, she grabbed a tie and handkerchief and placed the items on the counter.

Maxwell entered the items into the cash register and carefully folded each piece before placing them in a bag. Unable to maintain his poise he asked, "So, mystery lady, may I ask your name?"

"It's Lina," she replied, as she pulled a credit card from her wallet to pay for her purchase.

"Lina. A beautiful name for a beautiful woman." Maxwell looked at her credit card and noticed her name was spelled with an 'i' rather than the traditional 'e'. He held the card in his hand and looked up at Lina.

"Pardon me for staring at your card, but I noticed your name is spelled differently from what I'm used to."

"I get that reaction a lot. My name is African; it means tender."

Tender indeed, he thought. "Oh, I see." Determined to leave a good impression, Maxwell decided to slow things down. He didn't want to seem too eager. He completed her purchase and handed her the bag. "It was nice meeting you, Lina with an 'I'. And, hopefully I'll see you at church again."

Lina grabbed the bag and replied, "I'm sure you will. I enjoyed the service."

As quickly as she appeared, she was gone. Maxwell was grateful for the opportunity to meet Lina, but her purchase left him more curious than before. Who could that shirt have been for? More importantly, what was in that Victoria's Secret bag?

Chapter 4

Confident in her selection, Lina decided to spend a couple more hours browsing the shoe stores and specialty shops. She stood with fascination as she watched a young Asian woman shape a woman's eyebrows with a string. The woman's speed and precision entertained her.

She continued to casually stroll through the mall, hoping to find a good deal on shoes. Just as she sat down, her cell phone rang to the tune of *The Dream* by Shirley Murdock. Lina quickly retrieved the phone from her purse, looked at the name on the display screen, and pressed Accept.

"Hey, Mama. How are you doing?"

"I'm doing fine. How's my baby girl?"

"I'm good. I'm at the mall. I came to get daddy's birthday gift. He is going to love what I got him. I'll send it FedEx in the morning."

Lydia did little to mask her frustration. Lina noticed the change in her mother's tone. "What are you talking about FedEx? It's your father's sixtieth birthday. I know you haven't forgotten we're having a big celebration for him, and he expects to see his youngest child there. Plus, you know he has never gotten over your moving so far away." Pausing, Lydia softened her tone, "Especially in your condition."

Lina felt her temper rising. There was nothing she hated more than being reminded of her illness. "I am fine, mother," she sternly replied. "In fact, that's the reason I moved away. I refuse to sit around in misery while my family anticipates my death. I am too busy living to focus on dying."

"Lina, no one is here sitting around waiting for you to die. We're your family. We love you. Understand this, young lady, when everyone else seemingly turns their back on you, your family will be the ones to help pick up the pieces." Refusing to continue her conversation on a sour note, Lydia declared, "I'm not going to argue with you, that's not why I called. You go ahead and finish your shopping. I'll see you Friday. Be sure to call me and let me know what time your flight will be arriving." Secure in her assessment, Lydia continued, "I love you, baby, and one thing I know about my child, you love us way too much to disappoint us."

Lina's heart softened. Her mother was correct; she did love them too much to deliberately disappoint them. Besides, four hours travel time was well worth the joy she would see on her father's face. Exhaling gently, she replied, "I'll check with the airline when I get home. Kiss daddy for me, and tell him I'll see him in a couple of days."

After speaking with her mother, Lina no longer had a desire to shop. Lydia had a way of making her feel guilty. Walking out to her car, Lina reflected on her mother's words. The last thing she ever wanted to do was disappoint her father. Traveling to Durham was the least she could do. She hadn't been to her hometown in over a year. Excitement mounted as Lina thought about seeing her friends and family. She would appoint herself the designated photographer. It only seemed natural, seeing as though photography was her profession.

On the drive home, she thought about all she had missed in the past year. She expelled a soft giggle as her mind drifted to her sister, Zarion, who was now five months pregnant and sure to be freaking out about losing her athletic figure. Her brother, Gerald, had recently been honored with a humanitarian award for his work mentoring inner city youth. And, Javonne, her oldest sibling, was gaining notoriety for her café style restaurant in downtown Raleigh.

When Lina first moved to Chicago two years prior she made bi-monthly trips back to Durham in order to ease her parents' mind. Her father looked at her as though she was speaking a foreign language when she first told him she was taking all of her savings and moving to Chicago. He didn't like the idea of his youngest daughter moving to an extremely large city where she had no friends or family to look out for her. Lina cried as she struggled to convince her parents she was making the best decision for herself. Despite her compelling argument, her father, Joseph, never relented. Yet, with great despair, Lina stood by her decision. She felt in her heart, moving was the only way she would truly have peace.

The blaring of a car horn startled her. Consumed with her thoughts, she failed to realize the traffic light had changed to green. "No sense in reliving that nightmare," she declared. Determined to keep her mind clear, she pressed the power button on her car stereo and sang along to familiar songs on the radio until she arrived home.

Chapter 5

I can't believe I saw her. She was right here in my store, and I made myself look like a complete idiot. Maxwell replayed his conversation with Lina in his mind. *Why am I trippin' over this woman? This is not me. I am Maxwell Lee. Women are practically standing in line waiting for an opportunity to get to know me, and I'm sitting here driving myself crazy over a woman I don't even know.*

Maxwell tried to shift his attention to the paperwork that overloaded his desk, but thoughts of Lina served as a constant distraction. Determined to maintain his pride, he forced himself to focus. He gathered several invoices and entered them into his accounts payable file.

Simon tapped on his office door. "Max, you have a phone call on line one."

"Thanks, man." Maxwell stretched his arms wide, relieving the tension that had settled in his muscles. "This is Maxwell. How may I help you?"

"Hello, son." Marilyn's enthusiasm penetrated the phone line. "Are you working hard?"

"Never too hard that I can't stop for my best girl. What's going on, Ma?"

"I'm calling to make sure you didn't forget about dinner this evening. I cooked a lot of food."

"How could I forget. I've been looking forward to it all day," he lied. Maxwell had forgotten his promise to his mother about dinner. "I'll be wrapping things up here in about an hour, and then all roads lead to your house."

"Okay, baby. I'm going to call Jason and make sure he's still coming. You know how your brother is. You have to catch him when you can. I wish that boy would settle himself down and get stable like you. I keep telling him, a good woman is not going to put up with his foolishness. Bouncing around from job to job and woman to woman is going to play out before long."

Maxwell exhaled slowly. He was not in the mood for his mother's comparisons. Whenever she compared Jason to him, it started an instant argument. Maxwell loved his mother and brother dearly, but he refused to be in the middle of another one of their disagreements.

"Ma, please don't do this today. You know it will only upset Jason, which will in turn upset you. I personally am looking forward to a pleasant evening. Stop worrying about him. He'll be fine. The Bible says the prayers of the righteous avails much, so if we are both praying for him, things will certainly turn around."

"You're right, son. We'll just believe God," Marilyn agreed. "Listen, I'm going to let you get back to work. I'll see you soon. I love you."

After concluding his conversation with his mother, he prayed silently. *Lord, please let this evening go well.*

Maxwell grew tired of running interference between his mother and brother. Although he was younger than Jason, he often felt like he had to act like he was the older brother. As much as he loved his mother, he knew she could be unreasonable at times. For as long as he could remember, there seemed to be a feud between his mother and brother. Over time, he came to accept it as their way of life.

Leaning his head back, Maxwell reclined in the burgundy leather office chair and placed his feet on the large mahogany desk. Vigorously massaging his temples, he closed his eyes, repelling the apparent stress that threatened to take precedence in his mind. As if on cue, Maxwell sat up and picked up the phone to call Jason.

After several rings, Jason groggily answered. "Hello," he garbled.

Shaking his head in frustration, Maxwell said, "Man, get up. It's almost five o'clock and you still got your butt in the bed?"

"What you want, man? I had a long night."

"I bet you did," he mocked. Maxwell decided to get to the point of his call. He knew if he didn't make his point he and Jason would spend the next five minutes playing an unending game of verbal tug of war. "Have you talked to Mama?"

"Naw, man, I haven't talked to Ma," Jason repeated sarcastically. "Why, what's going on?"

"She said she was going to call you when I talked to her a little while ago. I can't believe she hasn't called."

Jason sat up on the bed and pushed back the covers. Stretching, he replied, "She probably did. But shoot, you know me, I will tune this phone out in a minute."

Maxwell rolled his eyes, displaying his obvious frustration with his older brother. "She cooked a big dinner and she wants us to come over there. I told her I would be there in about an hour, and I know you can do the same thing."

"Man, I don't feel like fooling with Mama like that today. I'm not in the mood."

"You know you're wrong. We only have one mother, and you and I both know you would be devastated if something were to happen to her."

"Calm down, Minister Lee. I'm just messing with you. Mama called right before you did. All she had to say was food, and she had my full attention." Jason laughed. "You're getting all sentimental, sounding like you're about to cry and everything. I had to hurry up and end this before you broke out your Bible and preached a sermon on how to treat your mother," Jason mocked.

Maxwell couldn't help but laugh. Jason was right. He had various speeches prepared for dealing with his brother regarding their mother. "Alright, you got me. I guess I'll see you at Ma's house."

"Yeah, man. I'll be there," Jason replied

Following his conversation with Jason, Maxwell returned to the sales floor to check on things. He observed Lola completing a sale at the cash register, while Simon measured a customer's shoulders for a tailored fit Jacket. Cory nodded his head to the beat of the smooth jazz playing through the store's speakers, while he straightened sweaters on the table at the front of the store. Maxwell was grateful to God for blessing him with such a successful business.

Throughout high school and college, Maxwell worked in retail stores with the hopes of one day owning his own. His determination kept him focused amidst the constant distractions of adolescence and young adulthood. Now, at the age of twenty-eight, he had built a lucrative business that afforded him a very comfortable lifestyle. The only thing missing was a wife to share it with. Although he was flattered by the attention he received from women both in the mall, and at church, it wasn't appealing to him. He was looking for a woman who would look beyond his positions and his possessions and love him for the man he was.

Maxwell had always been a man who strived for excellence. The woman who would ultimately bear his name would have to be extraordinary.

Chapter 6

Lina grabbed her laptop computer from the desk and logged on to the Internet. She briefly reviewed her emails before booking a flight to Durham. With her father's birthday only three days away, she was going to have to make some quick adjustments to her schedule.

"Since I'm sitting here, I might as well get some work done." Lina scanned the computer for her most recent photos. She smiled at the thought of having her childhood hobby become her career. Her photos had appeared in several well-known publications and galleries. She felt her greatest accomplishment so far was having her photos on display at the Art Institute of Chicago. She often visited the museum just to take a peek at her savvy signature, *Fairweather*, in the corner.

Although her life had been filled with many challenges, Lina was determined to lead a fulfilled life. Every morning without fail, she gave thanks to God for another day and read her favorite scripture, Philippians chapter four verse eight. She felt as though her spirit was being renewed daily.

Carefully examining each photo, Lina selected several shots to submit to the editorial staff of the magazines and newspapers she contributed to frequently. Her computer chimed indicating she had a new email message. The picture of a disfigured young lady invoked her curiosity. She could tell from the poor resolution the picture had been taken by an amateur, possibly someone the woman knew. Below the first picture was another picture of a young couple. The girl in the second photo wore a small tiara and held a bouquet of beautiful red roses. The young man next to her stood strong and confident with his arms around her, wearing a football jersey. The message that followed brought tears to Lina's eyes. She read slowly, taking in every word.

Hello, Miss Fairweather, my name is Victoria Essence. On a recent visit to Zahra Art Gallery downtown, I was drawn to a picture of women standing by the ocean. The women appeared to be from all walks of life. Some were young and seemed to be full of life, some looked as though life had been rough for them, and some were old and appeared to be nearing the end of their lives. What stuck out to me the most was the way each of these women had their arms stretched out towards heaven. They all seemed different in so many ways, but at the same time appeared to be the same, all reaching out to someone greater than themselves. I like to believe they were reaching out to God. Each woman with her own petition, but yet believing He would grant their individual requests.

Lina was in awe of the spiritual connection Victoria had with the picture. When she snapped the photo, in her heart she was reaching out with her own petitions. She continued reading.

As I stared at that photo, I was filled with wonder and hope. With what appeared to be perfect penmanship hidden in the corner, I saw Fairweather. Your name alone saturated my mind. It caused more thoughts to embed themselves within my subconscious. I stood in front of the photo so long that the gallery owner came to check on me. Imagine her surprise when she saw the tears streaming down my face. I asked her who the photographer was and she gave me a gallery brochure that contained your website information. I could hardly wait to get home to view your website and see what else you had done.

Your photos depict true, human life. They are intensely thought provoking and engaging.

Lina was used to receiving emails from admirers of her work, but there was something different about this message. She continued to read.

This leads me to my reason for contacting you. The pictures attached to this email are both of me. The first picture shows how I currently look. The second picture shows my boyfriend and me after I had been crowned homecoming queen at the University of Illinois in Chicago. With it being my senior year, I was ecstatic. Following the ceremony, Jeremy, the love of my life, proposed to me to which I gladly accepted. Unbeknownst to me that would be the last photograph I would take looking like that. In celebration, Jeremy and I, along with our families, went to Chanel's Restaurant to celebrate our engagement. When we left the restaurant, I settled into the passenger's side of the car eager to enjoy a quiet ride home. I drifted off to sleep, only to be awakened by the sound of screeching tires. You see, Miss Fairweather, we were hit head on by a drunk driver.

Lina gasped and covered her mouth with her hand. "Oh, my God," she whispered. She didn't expect that. Unable to pull herself away, she continued to read.

Jeremy suffered several cuts and bruises. I, on the other hand, was not as fortunate. My seatbelt malfunctioned and I was ejected from the car. I slammed head first through the windshield. I was in a coma for six months. When I woke up, the doctors took me through several psychological tests before I was allowed to see a mirror. My face was unrecognizable. I couldn't believe it, I was hysterical. The doctors told me they had performed several surgeries. However, they were unable to restore my face to its previous state.

Tears escaped Lina's eyes. She couldn't imagine what life

must have been like for Victoria with her being so young and enduring such a traumatic event.

My mother later told me Jeremy had made an effort to spend time with me constantly. She said he talked to me and read to me every day that I remained comatose. Once I got out the hospital, I sat down and talked to him. As you can see from the photo, Jeremy is a handsome man. I told him I knew he would have no problem finding a more suitable mate.

Jeremy held me tightly in his arms and told me I was more beautiful now than I had ever been. He said there wasn't a single woman in the world that could bring him the joy that he got from me. Not only did he want to proceed with the wedding, he had gone as far as to plan the ceremony. He showed me a storage box filled with everything from the invitations to the reception hall location and information.

That's so sweet. He must really love her. Lina thought.

Since my accident I have avoided mirrors and pictures. I couldn't stand the sight of myself. After I saw your picture in the gallery, I knew you were the one God was directing me to. I believe you can bring out the beauty I'm told I possess within. I also feel your pictures will help me accept my new appearance. I would like for you to photograph my wedding. The ceremony is to take place in five weeks. If at all possible, I would like to arrange a meeting with you. I will pay you whatever amount you choose. If you are available, you may contact me at 312-555-1010. I look forward to hearing from you soon. Sincerely, Victoria.

Lina allowed her tears to flow freely. What a wonderful man Jeremy must be to look beyond Victoria's flaws and see the beauty within her. Most men would have ditched her while she was still in the coma, but he instead chose to stand by her. Lina jotted down Victoria's phone number in her planner, along with a note to call her as soon as she returned from her weekend trip to Durham.

Chapter 7

Maxwell pulled up in front of his mother's house. It didn't matter that he had lived on his own for the past six years. The small, red brick house with the black shutters and black awning over the porch would always be home to him. With the precision of a trained driver, he parallel parked his SUV. He was careful not to scratch his three thousand dollar rims on the curb. As he approached the front door, he observed the perfectly manicured lawn and colorful array of perennials that bordered the house and walkway. Climbing the five steps onto the porch, he used his key to let himself in. Once inside, he maneuvered his way through the living room to find his mother in the kitchen.

"Hey, Ma," he said while wrapping his arms around her in a loving embrace.

"Hey, baby." Marilyn returned her son's hug. "I hope you're hungry, because I cooked plenty."

"I can see that," he commented as he looked at the fresh green salad, large pan of lasagna, and garlic bread sticks lying on the counter. Maxwell inhaled the aroma as he watched steam rise from the tantalizing dishes. "Jason better hurry up, because I'm hungry."

"What you in here saying about me, lil' bruh?" Jason charged into the kitchen and grabbed Maxwell in a headlock.

"Man, quit playing. Let me go," Maxwell barked as he struggled to free himself from Jason's firm grip.

"Let that boy go, Jason," Marilyn muttered while shaking

her head and laughing at her sons behave in the same manner as when they were teens.

"Say mercy and I'll let you go," Jason joked before releasing his arm from Maxwell.

"Man, you get on my nerves. Why don't you act your age? You're a grown man." Maxwell angrily straightened his shirt and tie.

Jason looked at him and laughed. "You're not getting angry are you, Minister Maxwell Lee."

Releasing a laugh of his own, Maxwell deepened his voice and replied, "The Bible says be angry but don't sin. I'm not sinning yet, but if you put your hands on me again that may not remain true."

Marilyn placed her hands on her hips and looked from one son to the other. "Come on here and eat. The food is getting cold. Both of you are just as silly as ever.

Each taking their seat at the round wooden table, they filled their plates and bowed their heads to offer a prayer of thanksgiving. Wiping his mouth, Maxwell looked at Jason and teased him. "Dog, Jason, I know you were sleep when I talked to you earlier, but did you have to get out of the bed and come straight over here. That old dingy, raggedy, t-shirt is so wrinkled it looks like you were sleeping under the mattress."

Man, shut up," Jason said sarcastically. "Just because you came over here dressed in a starched white shirt, looking like you're being choked by that crazy looking tie, don't mean nothing. At least I'm comfortable. You look like you're ready to explode. Those buttons on the front of your shirt are begging for mercy."

Maxwell rubbed his belly and laughed. "That's all right, I'm full and happy. Ma, you threw down on that lasagna."

"I'm glad you liked it. I figured if the food was good enough

I might actually get to see my sons more often. Y'all have just forgotten about your mama."

Throwing his hands up, Jason grunted, "Here she goes. I knew it was coming."

"Boy, be quiet. I haven't gotten started, yet. I'm just saying, I practically have to bribe the two of you in order to get you to come over here. It's not like either of you live that far from here. I should see you more often than I do."

Jason and Maxwell gave each other a knowing look. Jason pointed to his watch, signifying Marilyn's speech was right on schedule.

"What are you tapping on your watch for, Jason?" she asked, "At least Maxwell has a bit of an excuse. He works full time, and he's in the ministry. But, you, on the other hand, can't keep a job. If you weren't spending so much time laid up with those ole trashy women, you could make something of yourself. Here you are, thirty-one years old with nothing to show for yourself. Just like your good-for-nothing daddy."

"I knew it. See that's exactly why I barely come over here. You couldn't go a whole hour without having something bad to say about me. You claim to be so saved, but yet you treat me like you hate me. I might not go to church that often, but I know enough to know that when you're a Christian you're supposed to live like you have Christ living in you. You don't have a clue about what's going on in my life."

Marilyn rose angrily from the table, "What did you say to me? You may be grown but I will still knock you out."

Maxwell quickly interjected. As usual, it was up to him to run interference, and to restore peace between his mother and brother. "Hey, calm down. Ma, you know Jason is trying to get some things together." Turning to Jason he said, "And, Jason, you know Ma loves you. For you to even think, let alone say she hates you, is crazy. Now, come on. We've had a delicious meal, and God has blessed us to be together again. Let's not ruin it over nonsense."

Clearing dishes from the table, Marilyn waved her hand in resignation and walked over to the sink to prepare dishwater.

Jason shook his head in frustration, "Whatever, man, I don't have time for this. I got stuff to do. I'm about to go."

"Man, you ain't going nowhere until we finish cleaning this kitchen. You know the drill. When Ma cooks, we clean."

Marilyn left the kitchen, which allowed Jason and Maxwell to have some time alone. She hoped Maxwell could talk some sense into his older brother. If only Jason was more like Maxwell, then she wouldn't have to spend so much time in agony praying for him to straighten up. She couldn't understand where she went wrong. On one hand, she had a son that others would easily view as a loser. He couldn't keep a job, he lived in a rundown apartment in one of the roughest neighborhoods in Chicago, and he relied on public transportation. When he did get a car, it was in such poor shape that it couldn't even pass the emissions test. On the other hand, she had Maxwell, a very successful businessman. His store had gained national notoriety. He was a college graduate, and best of all he was a minister. The only thing he was missing was a beautiful bride. That was one thing she didn't even bother expecting from Jason. He was always with a different woman, each one trashier than the last. While sitting in her recliner, she thought back to Jason's words. Who was he to tell her she needed to live like she had Christ living in her. That was one thing she never worried about. She loved God above all else and it showed, or so she thought.

****

"Man, why do you let Ma upset you like that?" Maxwell asked. Every time we get together, it's the same thing. Some stuff you have to let go. You know Ma is going to say something about you. You should've learned by now to ignore it."

"That's easy for you to say. She doesn't treat you like that. I have been putting up with this since I was a kid. It seems like all my life Mama has been talking crazy to me. I'm not stupid. I know the reason she does it is because she can't stand my father. It makes me mad, because I don't have anything to do with that. I'm fed up. Mama don't know nothing about me. She thinks she knows me, but trust me, she don't have a clue."

Jason straightened the chairs around the table. "Did you ever call Maxine?"

"Naw, I got something else on my mind right now. I'll call her one day."

"What, or should I say who, you got on your mind?"

"Nothing, man, it's nothing. I'll call her."

"All right, dude. Do your thing. I'm just saying, you need to call her. I'm telling you, she got it going on. Trust me, you don't want to keep a woman like that waiting.

Frustrated at Jason's constant badgering, Maxwell firmly replied, "Like I said, I'll call her."

Maxwell dried and put away the last of the dishes. He picked up the containers Jason had stored the food in and placed them inside the refrigerator. Once the kitchen was finished, he joined his mother in the living room. Marilyn sat quietly, focusing her complete attention on the televangelist. Unwilling to mask her disapproval of her eldest son, she grunted as opposed to giving him a hug and kiss when he told her goodbye.

"Ma, why do you do that?" Maxwell asked.

Marilyn stared hard at Maxwell. "Do what? I don't know

what you're talking about."

Folding his hands, Maxwell sat back on the couch. "You know exactly what I'm talking about. Whenever we have a meal together, you always pick on Jason. I try to understand it, but I can't. One minute we're having a great time, and then out of nowhere you explode like a bottle rocket on the fourth of July."

Marilyn turned to face her son. "I know you don't understand. There are some things you can only understand if you are a parent. I did my best to raise you boys, and it's heartbreaking to see my son whom I love dearly throwing his life away. He could be so much better than he is, but he doesn't want that. Jason is content on being nothing."

"Ma, how could you say something like that about your own son? I may not be a parent, but I do know the word of God. In Jeremiah thirty-one and three, the Bible says 'with loving-kindness have I drawn thee.' If we are ever going to draw Jason to Christ, it is going to have to be through love. As long as he feels rejected by you, he is going to stray farther away. We have to be an example."

Unable to speak, Marilyn closed her eyes and whispered a silent prayer. Part of her wanted to tear down the wall that had been so firmly built by her. But, the reality of it all was Jason lived the way he did by choice. There was no way she was going to allow his lack of accomplishment to be her fault. She'd raised him the best she could. Now it was time for him to apply what he had been taught to his life, and be a man.

Chapter 8

Lina sat quietly on the plane anxiously awaiting the landing. The two and a half hour flight afforded her the opportunity to relax and read. Her life had been so full lately that reading was a luxury she hadn't been privileged to do. After completing her photography projects during the day, she was usually too tired to look at a novel, let alone read one. The plane bounced onto the runway with a thunderous roar. She gripped the armrest, firmly bracing for the slight impact.

Although she initially protested, the gentle vibration in her stomach revealed Lina's enthusiasm for her homecoming. Standing attentively in the baggage claim area, she looked for her maroon luggage with the gold scarf firmly tied around the handle. Within minutes, she secured her bag and headed out the door to the passenger pick up area. Gerald jumped out of the car wearing the smile of a proud, older brother. Without hesitation, he grabbed the bag out of her hands.

"Hey, baby girl. Let me take this off your hands."

Lina returned his smile. "Hey," she shrieked, wrapping her arms around him in a tight embrace. "What have you been doing? Looks like you've packed on a few pounds since I was home last."

Gerald opened the car door and looked at Lina with a menacing stare. "Girl, get in the car. You just got home and you're already starting."

The two exploded in laughter as Gerald pulled away from the curve. Traffic on 147 was light, allowing Lina the opportunity to admire the beauty of her hometown. The more things had changed, the more they stayed the same. Peering at the University campuses, she reminisced about her college days. As far away as she had gone, although temporarily, she was back where she had started.

"What's on your mind?" Gerald asked. "You're too quiet over there."

Lina turned her attention to her brother. "I'm just looking at how different, yet familiar, everything looks. I can't believe it's been over a year since I was home. I can't wait to see Mama, and Daddy."

"Trust me, baby girl, the feeling is mutual. Mama has been cooking all day, and I don't think it's a soul in Durham that she hasn't told that you were coming home."

Exhaling deeply, Lina expressed her frustration. "I hope all those folks don't come over today. I'm not in the mood for all that. I just want to have a quiet visit with my family."

"Now you know your visit is going to be anything but quiet." Gerald let out a soft giggle, "That's what you get for staying away so long."

Lina poked him in the arm with her elbow. "Be quiet. Nobody asked you for your two cents."

As Gerald turned the corner to Kenya Avenue, Lina's eyes widened. Seeing her parents' home caused goose bumps. She knew her acquired independence wouldn't mean a thing once she crossed the threshold. For the next few days, she would be their baby.

Once Gerald parked the car she quickly jumped out leaving him to carry her luggage. She couldn't wait to see her parents. Lina sprinted into the house through the open garage door. Entering the kitchen, she was greeted by the enticing aroma of hot peach cobbler.

"Mama, Daddy, I'm here," she yelled.

"In here, baby," Joseph eagerly replied.

Without hesitation, Lina joined her parents in the living room. Both were standing, waiting to greet their youngest daughter with open arms. Lina relaxed in her parents' arms as they shared a group hug.

Joseph reclined in his large, chocolate brown recliner. "Sit down, baby. How are you doing?"

Lina and her mother sat parallel to her father on the matching chocolate brown and tan sofa. "I'm doing good, Daddy. Business is going well. I have no complaints."

Lydia examined her daughter curiously. Reaching up, she smoothed Lina's curly, shoulder length tresses. "Are you really doing okay?" she probed. "You look as thin as a rail. Have you been eating and taking care of yourself like you're supposed to? Have you been taking your medicine correctly?"

Expelling air from her lungs roughly, Lina pulled her head from her mother's reach and stared her in the eyes. "Yes, Mother. I'm taking care of myself. Actually, I'm healthier than I have ever been. I passed my last physical with flying colors. My doctor was very pleased."

Not willing to start an argument, Lydia resigned. "Well, I still think you look as thin as a rail. That's okay, I'm going to fatten you up this weekend. Lydia tapped her daughter on the leg before rising from the couch and going to the kitchen.

"You know your mama is just concerned about you, baby girl. Don't get huffy with her."

"I know, Daddy. I meant no disrespect. Mama just goes over the top sometimes."

Joseph looked upon his child with great compassion. "That's love, baby. She only does it because she loves you. It's not easy having you live so far away from your family."

Lina smiled at her father. He was the designated go-between when Lina and her mother didn't agree. Gerald joined Lina and Joseph in the living room after placing his sister's bags in her bedroom. Within minutes, Lydia return with a tray carrying four bowls of hot cobbler, each topped with a scoop of vanilla ice cream.

"Ooh, Mama, that looks good," Lina exclaimed. Without hesitation, she grabbed one of the bowls and devoured her dessert.

"Dog, slow down, girl. Nobody's going to take it away from you." Gerald laughed at his sister.

Lina shared his laughed. "Oh, you be quiet," she replied. "You better hope I don't take yours from you. It's been a long time since I've had Mama's peach cobbler. I've missed this."

Lydia shook her head, laughing at her children. "Do the two of you know how to do anything other than fight?"

Gerald and Lina looked at each other and burst into laughter. Scraping the remnants of cobbler from her bowl, Lina gestured with her spoon. "When are Zarion and Javonne getting here?"

"They should be here in a little bit. They are both eager to see you." Lydia collected the empty dessert bowls from her family. "You should see Zarion. That girl is so round, it looks like she's carrying around a soccer ball in her shirt."

"I have got to see this. Little Miss Perfect Body, I'll bet it's driving her crazy."

"You know it is. I have to constantly remind her that she's pregnant and her belly is going to get bigger, whether she likes it or not."

"I brought my camera. I plan on getting some good pregnancy shots of her while I'm here. She might be mad at first, but she'll appreciate having the memories after the baby is born."

"Yeah, she will. I have pictures of all four of my pregnancies. I keep them in the photo album next to each of you all's baby picture."

The doorbell chimed loudly, interrupting the conversation. Gerald offered to answer the door, allowing Lina and her parents to continue conversing. Almost simultaneously, they were joined by both of Lina's sisters and her cousin, Erin.

Lina rose enthusiastically from the sofa and embraced each lady. She teasingly exaggerated the distance between her and Zarion. "I don't want to crush my little niece or nephew."

"Let me go," Zarion remarked, shaking side to side, and freeing herself from Lina's arms. "I am not that big."

"I know, I couldn't resist," Lina retorted.

Patting her round belly, Zarion said "Umm, umm. Mama, is that peach cobbler I smell? The baby has been craving your peach cobbler all week long."

Javonne shook her head and rolled her eyes, "Lina, do you see what we have to put up with all the time. That poor baby hasn't even been born yet, but it has more cravings and needs than anybody I know."

Zarion shot her a nasty look. "Shut up, Javonne."

"Y'all are a trip," Lina observed. "Hold on, I'll be right back." Lina went to her room and retrieved her camera. Pointing the camera at her sister, she said, "All right Zarion, say cheese."

"You better gone somewhere with that camera, girl. I am not taking any pictures." Zarion sat on the sofa and crossed her arms in protest.

Lina stood in front of Zarion. "Get up, Z. You are going to

be grateful for these pictures after you have the baby. These are memories you will want to cherish. Trust me."

Surrendering to her sister's request, Zarion stood and posed for pregnancy pictures. After taking pictures of Zarion, Lina continued to snap photos of the entire family.

"All right, Lina, that's enough pictures for one day. Put that camera up and let's go for a walk." Erin grinned at her cousin, hoping for a positive response. Growing up, she and Lina had been more like sisters than cousins. She was looking forward to spending some time alone with Lina.

"Okay, give me a second. I need to grab a jacket." Lina retreated to her room to grab her jacket and to put her camera up. Within minutes, she and Erin were headed out the door. Placing her hands in her pockets, Lina walked slowly, relishing the neighborhood she had grown up in, and the conversation with her cousin. It was important to her to value every moment of her life. She had experienced enough to know that life was precious, and tomorrow was not promised to anyone.

"So, girl, how have you been? I haven't talked to you in a while. You all big time now. You don't have time for your cousin," Erin teased.

Lina gave her a knowing glance, "The phone works both ways, little girl. The same way my phone has number keys on it, yours does too." Lina grabbed Erin's cell phone from the holster on her belt and slid it open. "See, just as I suspected. There are keys here. You could've called me. Unless, of course, you didn't realize this phone slides up to make a call."

"Give me my phone, with your silly self." Erin snatched the phone out of Lina's hand. "Always trying to be funny. You get on my nerves."

Lina placed her arm around her cousin's shoulder as they shared a laugh. "So what's been going on here? I know one thing that has not changed, you are still News Channel 5."

Erin immediately shared the latest gossip with Lina. She told her about all of their former classmates that had been married, divorced, and arrested. Solemnly, she looked at Lina and requested they have a seat on the steps of the neighborhood church. Puzzled by the sudden change in Erin's demeanor, Lina complied.

"What's up, girl? You're acting like you have to tell me something devastating."

Exhaling roughly Erin said, "I guess its all how you look at it. I'm not real sure how you're going to take this."

"Just tell me what it is. There isn't much I can't handle anymore."

"It's about Kaine. I don't think you've heard about what happened to him."

"To tell you the truth, Erin, I could care less about what has happened to him. Kaine is no longer a part of my life."

"Girl, he's no longer a part of anyone's life. He was murdered a couple of weeks ago."

Lina covered her mouth with her hand, displaying her surprise. She didn't know how to feel about the news of her ex-boyfriend's murder. What he did to her when they were together was beyond cruel, but she didn't wish death on him. Regaining her composure, she found her voice and asked, "What happened to him?"

"Well, after you left he went around doing the same thing to other women that he did to you. He has ruined so many lives. Anyway, he messed around and picked the wrong woman to mess with. She must have lost it because she walked up on him and point blank shot him in cold blood. That chick unloaded a 357 in him. She shot him in his head, and his chest. I heard she shot that brother execution style."

"Wow." Lina sat silently, processing the information Erin had given her. She felt compassion for Kaine's family, however she wrestled with her feelings concerning him. Inwardly she had always felt he should pay for what he did to her. Hearing that the man she was once deeply in love with was now dead was unsettling.

Rising from the steps, Erin said, "We can go back to the house now if you want to."

"Girl please, we can finish our walk. It ain't that serious." Lina stood and dusted off the back of her pants. "Tell me what's going on with you."

"Nothing. Like always, everyday it's the same routine. I like Durham, but I think about getting out of here all the time. Shoot, life is short. I want to experience some things. I've been thinking about coming to Chicago with you to check it out."

Lina understood how her cousin felt. "If you ever decide to make that move, give me a call. I'll help you any way I can. I will give you this piece of advice though. If you decide to come to Chi-town you better have a plan. Don't come trying to figure it out. Know what you're coming for and you'll succeed. Chicago is a big city and a huge difference from Durham. It's easy to get caught up if you don't know what you're doing." The cousins continued to carry on small talk until they returned to Lina's parents' home.

After everyone left, Lina went into her bedroom to relax. Lying upon her bed, she reflected on her conversation with Erin. She couldn't believe Kaine was dead. In a small way, she was envious of the woman that took his life. The unknown woman had the courage to do what Lina could only have thought about.

This is silly, she thought. She was capable of many things, but consciously taking a human life was not one of them. Grabbing her pillow in her arms and squeezing tightly, she silently prayed for Kaine's family until she was overcome by sleep.

Chapter 9

Maxwell frantically scanned the congregation, looking for Lina. He struggled to stay focused, but he was quickly losing the battle. After the choir completed their second selection, he surmised she would not be attending service that day. Pushing back feelings of disappointment, he offered his full support to Pastor James.

Upon the conclusion of the service, Pastor James pulled Maxwell aside. He placed his hand on Maxwell's shoulder and displayed a warm, fatherly smile. "Don't rush off, son. I want to talk to you a moment. Please join me in my office."

Maxwell hoped his lack of attention hadn't been evident during the service, but he assumed that much like an attentive parent, Pastor James had noticed. "Yes sir, Pastor. I'm right behind you."

Trailing along like a faithful student, he followed Pastor James to his study. The short hallway seemed to go on for miles. How could he, a minister, explain to his pastor his lack of attention stemmed from his focus on a woman. He should have been focused on the Lord, but he could only think about the woman whom he had only spoken to once. As much as he hated to admit it, Lina Fairweather had him mesmerized.

Pastor James opened the door to his study and offered Maxwell a seat in front of his desk. Taking his own seat behind the desk, Pastor James laid down his worn Bible. Running his hand over the weathered cover, he looked intensely at Maxwell. "You know, son, I have been in the ministry for over fifty three years. In that time, I have seen and experienced many things. Much like the parable of the sower Jesus gave in Matthew chapter thirteen, I've seen the effects of the Word of God on people. Some readily receive it, and then quickly fade away, and some grab hold to it and never let go."

Maxwell sat uneasily. Uncertain of what direction Pastor James was going in, he remained silent. His heart beat rapidly.

"Son, I've seen ministers both young and old come and go. You don't get to be as old as I am without being able to read people. Some of the ministers that have come through these doors did so for no other reason than to chase skirts. Married men as well as single ones. I'm telling you, I have seen it all. Nothing surprises me anymore." Pastor James shook his head in disgust.

Swallowing hard, Maxwell was overcome with guilt. *Lord, I'm sorry. Please forgive me.* He silently prayed.

Continuing, he leaned forward and folded his hands on the desk. Looking Maxwell square in the eyes, he spoke sincerely, "Minister Lee, I'm getting tired."

Concerned, Maxwell retorted, "Pastor, it's been a long day. You preached hard. We can finish this conversation some other time. You really should go home and get some rest."

Expelling a soft laugh, he replied, "Not that kind of tired, son. What I'm trying to tell you is I believe it is time for me to begin the process of retiring from the ministry. I've been seeking God for some time now concerning this matter. God has finally given me the release. Son, God is a God of order. Therefore, He wouldn't have given me the release without first making provisions for this house. When I sought the Lord concerning the person He would have to carry this ministry along, He placed you before me."

The shock on Maxwell's face could not be denied. His

mouth literally fell open, displaying his surprise. "I don't know what to say. Pastor, are you sure?"

"Of course I'm sure, son. I know when God is directing me to do something." Pastor James gave Maxwell a stern look. "I know His voice, and I know this is His will for Christ the True Vine."

Reclining in his chair, he continued. "Now, please don't misunderstand, this isn't something that is going to happen overnight. I won't actually be retiring for another year. During that time, I will be preparing you to take over. There are many things I have yet to teach you."

"Yes, sir. I appreciate that. I'm willing to learn everything I need to know." Maxwell felt as though an elephant had been lifted from his shoulders. There he was panicking, expecting a verbal rebuke from his pastor, but instead he found out he would soon realize his dream of becoming a Pastor.

"Don't get ahead of yourself, son. Allow God to process you. You see, many people look at what they perceive as glamour when it comes to Pastors. Please, hear me when I tell you there is no glamour in ministry. It's hard work, and only the strong in the Lord survive. I'm not going to sell you a fantasy. I will teach you the realities of what it means to be a Pastor. But, son, know this, in all the training that I give you, there are some things you will only gain through experience."

Maxwell nodded his head in agreement. Rising from his seat, he extended his hand to Pastor James. Pastor James firmly gripped his hand in response.

"Son, remember the steps of a righteous man are ordered by the Lord. Allow God to order your steps, and you will never fail. You will make mistakes, but if you fall, don't waddle; get up and move forward. Most importantly, pray without ceasing."

Stepping from behind the desk, Pastor James wrapped his

arms around Maxwell and prayed God's blessings upon his life. After praying for his successor, Pastor James instructed him to keep the purpose of their meeting confidential until he made the formal announcement to the congregation.

"Can I discuss this with my family, Pastor?"

"That'll be fine, son. Just don't discuss it with the members of the congregation. Now, if you will excuse me, Sister James is waiting for me." Pastor James grabbed his hat off the coat rack in the corner of the room and opened the door so that he and Maxwell could exit the office.

"Whew!" Maxwell exclaimed once he was secure in his vehicle and driving home. "I can't believe I'm about to be a Pastor. Thank you, Lord."

Chapter 10

"Hey Cheri girl, what you up to?" Lina adjusted the Bluetooth earpiece so that she could hear better.

"Girl, I ain't doing nothing, sitting here watching TV. When did you get home?"

"Late last night. I was having such a good time with my family that I decided to take a later flight."

Cheri sat up on the couch and adjusted the volume on the television with the remote control. "So I take it your dad had a nice birthday celebration. When you called me Saturday, I could barely hear you, with all the noise in the background. It sounded like there were a lot of people there."

"It was. We had a real nice turn out. I saw friends and relatives I hadn't seen in years. There was so much food that I think I gained ten pounds looking at it. My mother did a lot of cooking, and on top of that my aunts cooked a lot and brought it to the community center where the event was held."

"That's good. I'm glad to hear you had a good time. What are you about to do now?" she asked.

Lina flipped open her laptop and pressed the Power button. "It's time for me to get back to work, the vacation is over. I need to follow up with the young lady that emailed me about photographing her wedding."

"Are you talking about the one that was in the car accident?" Cheri inquired.

"Yeah, that's the one. I'm going to call her today and possibly set up a meeting with her and her fiancé."

"Okay, girl. You go ahead and handle your business. I'm going to get back to my show. Give me a call later. Maybe we can go get something to eat or catch a movie."

"A movie sounds good. There are several out that I want to see. I'll call you when I'm finished."

After completing her conversation with Cheri, Lina pulled up the email from Victoria in order to retrieve her contact information. *What made her choose me?* She pondered the thought before picking up the phone and dialing the number listed in the email.

Following a few short rings, a young lady answered the phone in a gentle tone.

"Hi, my name is Lina Fairweather. I'm trying to reach Victoria Essence." Lina spoke clearly, in a moderate, professional tone. She often used a different tone when she dealt with clients over the telephone. She was a firm believer in making great first impressions. One thing she could not stand was for someone calling to discuss business with her to speak unprofessionally.

"Miss Fairweather, hi this is Victoria. Thank you so much for calling. I wasn't sure I would hear from you. I know you're a very busy woman. I can't tell you how much I appreciate this." Victoria's excitement flowed through the phone line.

"Thank you, Victoria. You're too kind." Lina found herself blushing. She felt added pressure to meet Victoria's expectations. Victoria's request came with an awesome responsibility. She wanted Lina to help her to rediscover her beauty. Realizing she was prematurely panicking, Lina took a deep breath and focused her attention on the conversation.

"I'm sorry it took so long for me to get back with you, but I went out of town for a few days. I read your email, and I must admit I was deeply touched. My heart goes out to you. I can't imagine going through what you have experienced. On the other hand, I was elated to see how Jeremy showed his love to you, and most importantly stood by you during such a difficult time."

"Thank you, Miss Fairweather. I realize I am truly blessed."

Lina decided to redirect the conversation. "The reason for my call today is, I was wondering when would be a good time for me to meet with you and your fiancé. With your wedding being a little more than a month away, I figured the sooner we can meet, the better. I have some time available for the next few days."

"Jeremy has the day off today. Would this afternoon be too soon?"

"This afternoon will be fine. How about we meet around two o'clock at a location of your choice. Oh, and Victoria, please call me Lina."

"Okay, Lina. Two o'clock sounds good. We can meet at my house."

Lina jotted down the address and directions to Victoria's house and ended her call. Since her meeting was several hours away, she needed to prepare her presentation, and re-organize her portfolio. Whenever she met with new clients, she arranged her portfolio with photos that she had previously taken to reflect the type of pictures the potential clients were requesting. For her meeting with Victoria, she chose photos of previous weddings she had photographed. She also included some nature shots, and candid photos.

Once she had completed her portfolio, Lina decided to go downtown to deliver some of her latest work to a few of her clients.

Chapter 11

Maxwell walked swiftly, keeping up with the downtown pedestrians. The smell coming from Garrett's Popcorn Shop filled the air as he left the James R. Thompson Center. Checking his watch for the time, he was relieved to know he had a dependable staff to open the store and carry on in his absence. The sudden blare of sirens commanded his attention, inviting him to turn and identify the cause. Maxwell continued to walk placing his focus on what was behind him rather that what was before him. Without warning, he bumped hard into a fellow pedestrian causing her to drop her bag.

"I'm so sorry, Miss. Please excuse me," he apologized.

"Don't worry about it," she snarled without looking up.

"Lina?" he asked in disbelief.

Lina stood quickly to face the stranger. Exhaling roughly, she smacked her lips. "You. Unbelievable, this is absolutely unbelievable. Are you stalking me or something?"

"Not hardly," Maxwell shot back. "Haven't you ever heard of a coincidence? I happen to be taking care of some business today. I had no idea I would run into you, literally."

"Is that right?" Lina said, folding her arms across her chest.

"Yes, that is exactly right." Maxwell smiled sheepishly. "I will, however, confess that it's nice to see you, again. I missed you at church yesterday."

"How could you miss me at church? I've only attended one time. I don't think that qualifies me as a member."

"In that case, I should say I looked for you at church

yesterday. Is that better?"

"Is that so? Well, there sure isn't any harm in looking."

Maxwell stared deeply at Lina. "Miss Fairweather, why are you always so defensive. Do I bother you that much?"

"What are you talking about? I'm not defensive," she retorted.

"Yes you are. In fact, you're doing it again."

Lina inhaled and forced the air out through her teeth. "Doing what again? What are you talking about?"

"Being defensive. I assure you, Miss Fairweather, I mean you no harm." Maxwell smiled warmly, hoping to ease Lina's resistance. "Tell you what, since I practically knocked you off your feet, why don't you let me treat you to lunch. You can even pick the spot. We're already downtown, and there are a ton of restaurants you can pick from that are within walking distance. Then you won't have to feel uncomfortable getting into my vehicle."

Lina's first thought was to decline Maxwell's invitation. She didn't know him. She had only seen him a few times. However, the loud grumble in her stomach reminded her that she had skipped breakfast. "Why not? I could go for a bite to eat. We can go to Kerrie's Diner on State Street. The food there is delicious."

Maxwell couldn't avoid the huge grin that formed on his face at hearing Lina's response. He didn't expect her to accept the invitation, but he was pleasantly surprised that she did.

They walked in awkward silence to the diner as Maxwell studied her confident stride. For weeks, he had hoped for the opportunity to sit down and talk to her. Now that he had the chance, he didn't know what he would say. *Lord, you are going to have to help me with this. I don't know what to say,* he silently prayed.

The red and white checkered tables, and red, padded vinyl benches at the diner reminded him of a 70s sitcom. Servers moved quickly, some carrying round trays filled with hot meals, while others carried pitchers of water and pots of coffee. Small bells rang loudly, tapped by the cook to notify the servers of completed orders.

Maxwell briefly scanned the menu as a formality. He had already decided on his meal when he saw a waitress carrying a plate with a gooey steak and cheese hoagie. He listened attentively while Lina placed her order.

"Why do you have that big cheesy grin plastered all over your face?" Lina asked sarcastically.

"I was just thinking, you are a woman after my own heart. To be honest with you, I was waiting to see if you were going to do like most women and order a garden salad for the sake of appearing modest in front of a man. But you surprised me ordering that double cheeseburger and fries. As small as you are, I don't know where you put it all."

"Please, I don't have time for being phony. This is me, the real deal. In my opinion, this world would be a much better place if people would just be who they are and not spend their time focusing on trying to impress people. Once you start an act, it can be hard to keep it up. Eventually, they slip up and their true colors show."

Raising his hands in surrender, Maxwell replied, "I can agree with you on that." The more Maxwell looked at Lina the more things he noticed about her. He wasn't sure why, but the woman in front of him left him mesmerized. It wasn't that she had done anything special to warrant his adoration. She was genuine, and that made her the most desirable woman in the world to him. He could no longer stand the suspense of wondering who the guy was Lina had bought the gifts for at his store.

"So, how did your friend like the gift you bought him?"

Lina looked puzzled. Had this guy really been stalking her? Why was he so overly concerned about her life? "What are you talking about?" she asked.

"Forgive me; I guess I should have gone into a little more detail. Did your friend like the shirt, tie, and cufflinks you bought?"

Embarrassed by her own ignorance, Lina expelled a soft giggle. "It's funny that you should mention that. I can't say that he's ever been referred to as my friend, but I guess he could be considered that." Lina could tell Maxwell was phishing for information about her. She decided to play along. "To answer your question, yes he did like it. He liked it very much, actually, and the fit was perfect. In fact, he looked like a million bucks wearing it." Turning the interrogation on to him she asked, "Now I have a question for you. Do you normally make it a practice to follow up with your customers outside of the store concerning their purchases?"

Maxwell couldn't help but to smile. "I only follow up when I get the opportunity. I like to make sure my customers are satisfied."

Lina crossed her arms and gazed curiously at Maxwell, "Is that right. I see now."

Changing the subject, Maxwell decided to dig deeper. Since she didn't wear a wedding ring, he figured she wasn't married. "Okay, Miss Fairweather, you know quite a bit about me. Tell me a little bit about yourself. For instance, what do you do for a living? Do you have any siblings? Are your parents alive? Do you have any children?"

Lina looked at Maxwell as if she was standing before a firing squad. "Darn, slow down. Is this an interview?"

Maxwell laughed, "No, it's not an interview I'm only trying to get to know you. Why do you ask? Does it feel like an interview?"

"Yeah, it does," she replied, sharing his laugh.

"I'm sorry, I didn't mean to grill you. I imagine it did sound like an interrogation." Maintaining focus, he continued. "If you don't mind, I would like to know the answers."

Resting her back against the booth, Lina folded her hands on the table and began answering each of Maxwell's questions. "Let's see. I am a freelance photographer. In fact, my camera was in the bag you knocked out of my hand. For your sake I'm glad it was in a protective case," she teased before continuing. "My work can be found in several publications as well as some galleries. I'm the youngest of four children. I have a brother and two sisters. My parents are both alive and still together, and no, I don't have any children."

The waitress returned and placed their meals on the table. "Mmm, this looks delicious." Once their waitress had left the table, Maxwell pushed his plate aside. "Lina, if you don't mind, I would like to bless our food before we eat."

"By all means, please do," she gladly responded.

Maxwell offered a short prayer of thanks before diving into his steak and cheese sandwich. They continued to engage in light conversation as they consumed their meals. Maxwell was pleased to see Lina smile as they conversed. She appeared to be more relaxed around him, which was comforting because he hoped to see her again.

Lina stirred the ice in her glass of water with a straw before taking a sip. "Thanks for inviting me to lunch. It was a very kind gesture."

"You're welcome. Maybe we can do this again sometime."

"Perhaps, only time will tell," she replied.

"I guess we better get out of here." Maxwell paid the check and placed a tip on the table for the waitress. Once they were outside, he extended his hand to Lina. "I enjoyed myself, Miss Fairweather."

"I did too. You had some pretty interesting ministry stories. The one about the choir member's hat falling off and rolling through the pulpit while she was playing the tambourine was too funny. I'll bet that poor woman was so embarrassed."

"If she was, she hid it well. In fact, if my memory serves me correctly, she was laughing harder than anybody. You have to know her to understand. She laughs at everything."

"I can imagine. It had to have been pretty funny." Lina looked at her watch. "I should get going. I have a few projects I'm working on that I need to finish. I had a nice time."

Maxwell nodded his understanding. "Before you go, I was wondering if we can exchange telephone numbers."

"I guess that will be alright." Lina reached into her bag, pulled out her business card, and handed it to him.

"Thanks." Maxwell accepted her card and offered her one of his own. After saying their goodbyes, they parted in different directions. Maxwell stepped as though he was walking on clouds. Lina was like a breath of fresh air for him. He could hardly wait for them to meet again.

Chapter 12

Maxwell walked into the store whistling. He greeted each of his staff members with huge smiles and a friendly wave. On the way to his office, he stopped briefly to straighten shirts hanging on the rack. The employees all eyed each other curiously, like they were wondering what had caused Maxwell to be so cheerful. They reasoned together, each developing their own theory.

Simon stopped in mid-sentence to admire the beautiful woman that entered the store. Her long, flowing tresses mesmerized him. Her lipstick glistened as though it had been freshly applied. She wore what appeared to be a tailored business suit with a skirt that revealed toned, shapely legs. Cory reached over and pushed Simon's chin up, closing his mouth. Each of them stared aimlessly as the mysterious woman approached them. Finding his voice, Simon offered the customer assistance.

"Hello, gentlemen." She spoke seductively, "I'm looking for the owner, Maxwell Lee. Is he in by any chance?" she asked.

"Just a moment, I'll get him for you." Simon rushed into Maxwell's office without knocking.

Maxwell sat at his desk reminiscing about his time spent with Lina. He debated about how soon he would call her. Startled by Simon's sudden entrance, he looked up and frowned. "Man, why are you busting up in here like that? Is there a fire or something?"

Realizing he had scared Maxwell, Simon laughed. "No, it's

nothing like that. There's a woman here to see you. Man, she's fine too."

Had Lina come to the store? Maxwell thought, and then quickly dismissed the idea. He looked at Simon confused. "Who is she? Is she a customer, a vendor, or what?"

"I don't think so, not with the way she came up in here."

Maxwell's forehead wrinkled. "Send her in, I guess. I don't have a clue who it could be."

Simon returned to the sales floor and escorted the woman to Maxwell's office.

The woman stood in front of Maxwell's desk and dropped her purse in the chair. "So you can't call nobody, huh?"

"What's up, girl." Maxwell enthusiastically rose from his seat and embraced Maxine.

"You're not getting off that easy; in here acting like you're all excited, but yet you couldn't call me. I know Jason gave you my phone number."

"Girl, quit playing and give me a hug. I was going to call you. I just haven't had the opportunity yet."

"Yeah, right." Maxine returned his embrace. He offered her a seat and returned to his seat behind the desk.

Leaning back in his chair, Maxwell crossed his legs and folded his arms. "So, tell me how you've been? What's been going on?"

"Not much, working hard, and going to church. My life is basic. I spend most of my time either at home, work, or church."

"What's a pretty lady like you doing leading such a basic life? I would have thought you would be married with children by now."

"I beg your pardon. I could say the same thing about you. I can't believe a woman hasn't scooped you up by now. Jason was telling me, you got it going on. You got this store, your own townhouse, and you're a minister. You, sir are a rare commodity. So why are you single?"

Maxwell looked at Maxine oddly. She sounded like she was reading his resume. "Since you put me on the spot like that, I'm single because I choose to be single. I have seen too many marriages end in divorce. I'm waiting to find the wife that God has destined for me. I refuse to settle. That, my dear is why I'm still single."

"Touché, I can't argue with that." Maxine shifted in her seat and crossed her legs. "It appears that after all these years we still have some things in common. That's also why I'm single. I too refuse to settle. I came close to getting married once, but it didn't work out. I found out he was cheating on me a few weeks before the wedding. After that, I became extremely guarded. I don't want to be hurt again."

Nodding his head in agreement, Maxwell replied, "I can relate." He looked directly at Maxine and questioned, "What brings you by here today?" He was trying not to appear rude, but her sudden visit made him curious. He was glad to see her, but he could only seem to focus on Lina.

Maxine ignored Maxwell's bluntness. She could tell he was a bit distracted, but it didn't faze her. He was a good catch, and she wasn't going to let him slip through her fingers. He represented everything she wanted in a man. He was handsome, financially secure, and a minister. There was no way she was going to miss out on Maxwell. The fact that they were childhood friends gave her a slight advantage. She would use their history as a means of getting closer to him.

"Can't a girl stop by and visit with her friend? I've wanted to get by here for some time now. I got out of court early today and that afforded me the opportunity to drop by." Maxine shifted in her seat, and crossed her legs. "Why don't we grab a bite to eat? Do you have lunch plans?"

"I'm sorry, I can't. I had an early lunch today. I'm not hungry at all. Maybe we can do it some other time."

Maxine poked her mouth out, expressing her disappointment. "In that case, how about dinner tonight? I haven't seen you in years. I'm eager to catch up and find out what has been going on with you."

Maxine was persistent, so Maxwell surrendered. "I'm not sure what time I'll leave here tonight, but I tell you what, I'll call you when I get ready to leave and we can get together later. Will that work for you?"

"Yes, that'll be fine." Maxine reached in her purse and pulled out a business card.

He quickly retrieved the card from her hand. "Maxine Miller, Esquire, specializing in Business and Real Estate law," he read aloud. "I'm scared of you."

"As you should be," Maxine responded seductively. "I'm the best, Chicago has to offer."

"I heard that," he replied while escorting her to the door.

After receiving a final hug, she left.

The smell of Maxine's perfume lingered in his office long after she was gone. He shook his head in bewilderment. He had always been turned off by pushy women, but ooh wee, Maxine was fine. *I may be a minister, but I am single and I'm sure not dead*, he thought. What was he thinking? Maxine was an old friend. Looking at her he was sure she had men lined up to be with her. He dismissed the idea of her coming on to him.

Chapter 13

Lina sat quietly in the sanctuary trying to avoid Maxwell's intent stare. She'd noticed a few missed calls on her cell phone during the week but didn't think much of it. The last thing she wanted was to get involved with someone. She still felt the pain of Kaine's betrayal. Every day of her life served as a constant reminder of what she had endured. Lina enjoyed the services at Christ the True Vine, and she was not willing to have anyone change that.

"Girl, what's going on with you and Minister Lee?" Cheri asked quizzically.

"I don't know what you're talking about," Lina retorted. "There ain't nothing going on between us. Why would you even ask me something like that anyway? All I'm doing is sitting here enjoying the church service." Lina folded her arms across her chest and pouted.

Cheri stared quizzically at her friend. She'd never known Lina to snap like that over something so insignificant. It was totally out of her character. She had only been joking with Lina, but now she was beginning to wonder if there was something Lina wasn't telling her.

"I was only joking. He hasn't stopped staring at you since we sat down. But since you got all huffy with me, you're making me wonder. You don't snap like that over nothing. Now give up the goods. What is it that you're not telling me?"

Lina shrugged her shoulders. "There's nothing to tell. Now can we please focus on the service? I'm trying to hear the pastor."

"Yeah, okay. You're trying to hear the pastor all right. This is not over." Cheri folded her arms and crossed her legs in protest. There was no way she was going to let this slip by.

At the conclusion of the service, Cheri grabbed Lina's arm and pulled her towards the door. She was determined to find out what Lina was keeping from her. The aisles filled quickly with people making it difficult for them to leave.

Maxwell noticed Lina approaching the exit. He moved quickly to stop her before she could leave.

"Hello, ladies. How are you today?" he asked without taking his eyes off Lina.

Cheri leaned in front of Lina, gaining his attention. "We're doing fine, Minister Lee, and you?"

Maxwell tried to mask his embarrassment. "Please forgive me, Cheri."

"Yeah, you're forgiven." Cheri replied sarcastically. "It's obvious you're not interested in a conversation with me, so I'll excuse myself." She walked away and looked back at Lina.

"Cheri," Lina exclaimed. She couldn't believe Cheri had put Minister Lee on the spot like that. She had been known for her lack of decorum at times, but that was tacky even for Cheri. Lina rolled her eyes at Cheri before giving her the familiar, *I'm going to kill you* look.

Giggling at her friend's obvious discomfit, Cheri waved goodbye and exited the sanctuary.

Turning her attention to Maxwell, Lina raised her hand. "I'm sorry. Please excuse my friend. Sometimes she tends to act as if she has no home training. I honestly don't know what I'm going to do with her."

"There's no need to apologize. Cheri is only speaking

her mind. To be honest with you, at times I wish there were more blunt people in the world. Maybe there would be less speculation if people said what was really on their minds."

Maxwell smiled admiringly at Lina. Every time he saw her, she looked more beautiful than the time before. She could wear a t-shirt and overalls with her hair in a ponytail, without wearing any makeup and still be beautiful to him.

"I tried to call you last week, but I figured you must have been pretty busy since I didn't get you. How are things going? How did your meeting go with the engaged couple? Did you decide to shoot their wedding? What about..." Maxwell noticed the blank stare on Lina's face. "I'm sorry, I'm just babbling on and on."

"Now there's something we can agree on," Lina smirked. "You've asked me so many questions that I'm not sure what to answer first. Let's see, things are going fine. The meeting with the engaged couple went great. I'm shooting their wedding in a little over a month. They were such a beautiful couple. I couldn't turn them down if I tried."

Maxwell felt like a teenaged boy struggling to gain the attention of the popular girl in school. "I'm glad to hear that. Their story was so compelling when you told me about them at the diner. I was oddly drawn to them. I've found myself thinking about them and praying for them at the oddest times."

Lina noticed her conversation with Maxwell had gained several spectators. Some of the congregants were subtle in their snooping, while others boldly watched unashamed. *I don't have time for this drama,* Lina thought. She was not the type of woman to go to church looking for a man, and she was not going to allow herself to be labeled as such.

She pulled her purse strap up on her shoulder and moved her Bible from one hand to the other. "Maxwell, it has been nice talking to you, but I really must go, I have a ton of things I need to get done."

Confusion caused Maxwell's forehead to crease. He wondered why there was a sudden shift in Lina's demeanor. Quickly glancing around the room, he understood. "I'm sorry, I didn't mean to take up so much of your time. I appreciate you talking to me for as long as you did. If it's okay with you, I'd like to continue this conversation over the phone. When would be the best time to call?"

Lina pondered the thought. Looking at Maxwell, she could see the sincerity in his eyes. He seemed genuinely interested in her. Although she didn't share his feelings, she felt she could at least entertain the thought of establishing a possible friendship with him.

"Sure, why not," she said with a hint of hesitation. "You can call me pretty much any time. If I don't answer, leave a message, and I'll call you back."

"Ok, great," Maxwell was ecstatic. He knew that if he could get Lina to talk to him, then he could surely tear down the obvious barrier she had placed between them. "Then, I'll give you a call soon."

Lina left the sanctuary. Cheri was waiting for her outside. Cheri grabbed Lina by her arm and walked with her towards her car. Lina was prepared for Cheri's third degree questioning. There was no way Cheri would drop the subject, so Lina decided it would be easier to cooperate.

"Okay, Miss Lady. Give up the goods. There is obviously something going on between you and Minister Lee." She tried to read Lina's expression but Lina held her composure well. Pointing her finger at Lina, she continued, "Oh, yeah and just in case you want to try to leave something out, I have all day. I know where you live, I *will* follow you home." Cheri stated while rolling her neck.

Nonchalantly, Lina met her friend's gaze, "There really isn't anything to tell. We had lunch together one time and that was it, end of story."

"Whoa, back up. What do you mean, you had lunch together? When did this happen, and more importantly why am I just finding out? I can't believe you would keep something this major from me."

"It happened last week. We were downtown. Excuse me, let me correct that before you flip out. I was downtown and Maxwell bumped into me, literally, and almost knocked me down. He felt bad about it, so he invited me to join him for lunch. I wanted to say no, but, girl I was so hungry I didn't know what to do. We walked to a nearby diner, talked, ate, and left. That's it. Nothing to write home and tell mom about."

Turning her lip upward, Cheri hummed, "Uh huh, "Maxwell, huh? So, I guess you and Maxwell are on a first name basis. I'll take that for now, but I still think you're holding out on me."

"Cheri, you know me. A man is the furthest thing from my mind right now. I've got too much going on in my life to even think about a relationship. Trust me, if there was anything to tell, you would've been the first one I told it to."

Lina reached up and gave her friend a hug. "Now, can I please go home? My dogs are barking."

"I told you about wearing those *cute* shoes," Cheri teased, "I'm telling you, girl, they're going to be the death of you."

"Forget you, Cheri. You always got something smart to say," she laughed. "Be careful going home, I'll talk to you later."

Chapter 14

Contemplating whether or not to call Lina, Maxwell sat in his recliner gazing at the numbers on his cell phone. On one hand, he didn't want to seem overly anxious, but he also didn't want to procrastinate too long and make her feel he wasn't interested. He scrolled through his Contact list until he located her phone number. Just as he was about to press the Send button, his phone vibrated notifying him of an incoming call. Unable to identify the caller by the number displayed, Maxwell cautiously answered.

"Hello."

"Hey, Max, it's Maxine. How are you doing?"

"What's up, Maxine. I'm fine, how are things going with you?"

"Okay, I guess. I have been extremely busy lately so I must apologize for not speaking with you sooner. I'm really sorry about dinner the other night. When I saw you at the store, I had just finished a major case. But, once I got home, my assistant called me and told me the judge wanted to see some additional documentation."

"I understand. You didn't have to explain. Things happen."

"You're sweet," Maxine flirted. "So what have you been up to since we last spoke?"

Maxwell was not in the mood to talk to Maxine. His lack of interest was evident in his tone. "Not much. The same ole, same ole."

"I know what you mean," she countered. "Things are

pretty busy on my end with work and all." Maxine detected Maxwell's distance, however she had a plan, and nothing was going to keep her from achieving her goal of making Maxwell her own. He fit the bill of what she was looking for perfectly. Besides she didn't have the time, or the patience to start over prepping another man. She had an immediate need, and like it or not, Maxwell was going to fulfill it.

Unable to continue the charade, Maxwell decided to cut his conversation short. "I appreciate you calling me, Maxine, but I was just about to make an important call. Would you mind if I gave you a call back?"

"Okay, but before you go, I was wondering when I can redeem my rain check for dinner. Since we were unable to go out the other night, I really would like for us to get together and catch up."

"I can't say for sure right now. Between running the store and my commitment to the church, it's hard to give you a specific date. But don't worry, we'll come up with something. It was good hearing from you. I'll talk to you later, goodbye." Maxwell ended the call before Maxine could utter a response.

Staring at the receiver, Maxine fumed. It appeared things were not going to be as easy as she had originally anticipated, but she was far from discouraged. It was time for her to step up her game.

Shaking his head in frustration, Maxwell exhaled roughly. He didn't want to be rude to Maxine but he had other things on his mind right now, Lina in particular.

Returning to his Contact list he quickly selected Lina's number and pressed Send. Soft music played in the place of a standard ring.

"Hello, Lina Fairweather."

Lina's soft voice sounded melodious to Maxwell. "Hello,

Miss Fairweather. How are you today?"

"I'm fine," she replied. Following a brief awkward silence Lina continued. "I'm sorry, who is this?" she asked.

"I guess it would be unfair for me to assume you know my voice," he laughed. "This is Maxwell Lee. Did I catch you at a bad time?"

"Oh, it's my friendly neighborhood stalker," she joked. "Your timing is fine. After all, I don't really have a choice when it comes to you anyway. If I don't talk to you now, I'll end up bumping into you at the grocery store or something."

Impressed by her response, Maxwell remarked, "It's like that, huh. Okay, I see how you are."

"I'm kidding with you. Stop being so sensitive, Mr. Lee."

A smile creased Maxwell's face. His bout of nervousness faded. He initially wasn't sure how Lina would receive his telephone call, but she appeared to be happy to hear from him. "You have to give me some credit. You told me Sunday that it would be okay for me to call. I waited until Tuesday to do it. A real stalker would have called you thirty minutes later."

"Yeah, sure. I'll give you some credit. Unfortunately, my arm isn't long enough to reach out and pat you on your back," she teased.

"Very funny, Miss Fairweather. Tell me something. Are you always so sarcastic, or are you just doing it for my benefit?"

"Naw, this is pretty much how I am. I will admit it does tend to intensify when you're involved."

"Girl, you are a trip. I knew there was something special about you."

Maxwell and Lina talked for several hours. Their conversation covered everything from their music and movie choices to their views on fashion and automobiles.

They discussed their families, and career choices. Both were impressed by the ease of which they were able to talk to one another.

Lina tried to mask her yawn. She looked at the clock in surprise. "I can't believe it's almost ten o'clock. Time has really gotten away from us."

"I'm sorry," Maxwell countered. "I didn't mean to keep you this long. We have been talking for almost three hours."

"I know. I sure hope you are not as long winded in the pulpit as you are on the telephone," she teased.

"Aw, you're wrong for that."

Maxwell's robust laughter awakened feelings in Lina that she had long since buried. She didn't know what it was about him, but Maxwell had a way of getting to her.

"Lina, I can't tell you how much I have enjoyed talking to you today. I've learned a lot about you. Miss Fairweather, you truly are a special woman."

"Thank you, Maxwell. It has been really nice talking to you as well. I had better get off this phone. I have an early morning tomorrow. "

"I understand." Just as Maxwell was about to hang up, he changed the direction of the conversation. "Lina, I would really like to take you out sometime. Would you consider having dinner with me one night this week?"

Lina wasn't at all surprised by his proposal. Maxwell had been consistent in his pursuit of her. It seemed only natural for him to request a real date. "Dinner would be nice. When did you have in mind? My schedule is pretty full," she exaggerated.

"I promise I won't monopolize your time. How about we get together, say…Thursday."

Lina considered his offer. It had been a long time since she went on an official date. "You know what, that sounds like a good idea. Thursday would be good. I'm even going to let you pick me up. What time should I be ready?"

Maxwell almost dropped his phone. He had hoped Lina would say yes, but he didn't really expect it. "I'm sorry about that shuffling noise, the phone almost slipped out of my hands. I'll pick you up at six. That is, if it's okay with you."

Lina couldn't stop laughing. "Six o'clock is fine. Give me a call on Thursday and I will give you directions to my apartment. I'll see you then."

"Will do," Maxwell replied. "You have a good night."

"You too."

Lina continued holding the phone long after ending her call. She found herself smiling as she replayed their conversation in her mind. Maxwell was turning out to be a nice guy. After placing her phone on the charger, she quickly prepared for bed. Although he had made a good impression on her, Lina knew she couldn't relax her guard. No matter what, she could not allow Maxwell to get to her. She couldn't let him penetrate the wall of defense she had built. It was best for both of them.

Kneeling beside her bed, Lina began to weep softly. Her past mistakes lingered in her memory, reminding her of her sadness and her situation. Tears ran down her face, meeting under her chin before dropping to collect on her nightgown. "Lord, please help me. Why did my life have to go in this direction," she questioned. "Have mercy on me, dear God. I just want to be normal again. I just want the opportunity to be happy." Silence filled the room as her prayers felt unanswered. Exhausted, Lina climbed into bed and laid in anguish until sleep overtook her.

Chapter 15

"Amazing." Maxwell raised his head as he carefully maneuvered the razor over his neck and chin. Wiping the excess shaving cream from the razor, he splashed water over his face to clear the remnants of cream from his face. He shook his head in bewilderment as he reflected on his conversation with Lina the night before. She seemed genuine, unlike many of the women he had come in contact with in the past. Maxwell admired the ease with which he could talk to her. He felt like he was talking to one of his best friends.

Maxwell dressed quickly; he'd planned to stop by his mother's house before opening the store. Walking into the closet, he found the black and navy blue alligator shoes that were the perfect accent to his black slacks and navy silk shirt. A black necktie with splashes of navy completed his ensemble. He grabbed a thin black jacket as he headed out the door. Once outside, he took a deep breath to fill his lungs with the fresh spring air. The warmth of the sun rested upon his face.

Within twenty minutes, he pulled beside the curb, parking his vehicle in front of his mother's house. Marilyn stood outside in the front yard chatting with her next door neighbor. Both ladies held a cup of coffee in their hands.

"Who are you all gossiping about this early in the morning?" Maxwell teased.

"Excuse me?" Marilyn quickly replied, giving Maxwell a threatening stare.

"Calm down, Ma. I was just kidding." He laughed. "How

are you this morning, Ms. Betty?"

"I'm fine, Maxwell," she replied smiling.

Maxwell walked past his mother into the house. Laying his jacket on the couch, he made his way into the kitchen. The scent of freshly baked muffins and coffee filled the air. Grabbing a warm blueberry muffin, he cracked it open and placed a slice of butter inside. After preparing his cup of coffee, he made his way over to the table. Marilyn came inside and joined him with a muffin of her own.

"Who is she?"

Smiling broadly, Maxwell replied, "Who is who? I don't know what you're talking about?"

"Don't patronize me, son. You're in here eating, and humming, tapping your feet under the table. I know you well enough to know that some woman has you doing backflips. Now who is she?"

Maxwell exploded into laughter. "I'm just happy in Jesus, Ma."

Shaking her head, Marilyn looked him square in the eyes and said, "Try again."

Surrendering, Maxwell shared with her his interest in Lina. He spoke about how he first saw her at church and their chance meeting at his store. He told her about him almost knocking Lina over downtown, their lunch together, and finally their three-hour telephone conversation.

Marilyn smiled as she watched her son light up with excitement while he spoke of Lina. With each word, his smile grew broader. As a mother, she was cautious. She didn't want to see him get hurt, but she trusted her son. Maxwell had always been a responsible man. Unlike Jason, she knew Maxwell would make the best choices for his life.

"So when do I get to meet this woman that has your nose wide open?" Marilyn teased.

"Aw, Ma, come on. My nose is not wide open. Besides, nobody even uses that expression anymore." Maxwell rose from the table and placed his mug and saucer in the kitchen sink. Returning to the table, he took a seat opposite his mother. "I can't say for sure when you'll get to meet her. We haven't even had our first real date. Let me get to know her first, before you run her off," he laughed.

"Very funny," Marilyn replied, poking her lips out in protest. "I haven't run anyone off yet. And I can't help it if I don't bite my tongue. If I see something that is not right, I'm going to say something. It wouldn't be me if I didn't." Rolling her eyes, she continued, "Huh, you and your brother get so caught up in eyes and thighs that you lose focus on what matters most."

Maxwell raised his hands in surrender. "Okay, on that note, I'm going to head to the store. The mall will be open soon, and I have a ton of work to get done. Lina and I are supposed to go out tomorrow night. I'll give you a call and let you know how everything goes." Rising from his chair, Maxwell leaned over and kissed his mother on the top of her head, grabbed his jacket and left.

Once he was secure inside his vehicle, he cranked up his radio and sang along with the gospel melodies that poured from the speakers. He was determined that no matter what, he would not let his mother get to him. He was too excited about his date with Lina to let her ruin it for him. The conversation he had with Lina, revealed a lot about her. He was sure their first date would be a night she would never forget.

After a short drive, Maxwell arrived at the shopping mall. He pulled his vehicle around to the Merchant Only parking lot. He quickly checked his appearance and headed for his store.

"What's up, lil bruh," Jason yelled from across the parking lot. He was wearing a blue work shirt and navy blue work pants. Maxwell stood still, allowing Jason to catch up to him. "What's going on, Jason? What are you doing here this early in the morning?"

"You know me, man. I'm getting my hustle on."

"What do you mean, hustle? I thought you were working at Midway."

"Yeah, man. I'm still working at the airport, but you know me, I gotta get that paper." Jason tapped his hands together, emphasizing his point.

Maxwell forced his hands in his pockets and looked Jason in his eyes. "All right, man. So what's up? What is this new hustle of yours?"

Jason laughed at the seriousness of Maxwell's tone. "Chill out, Max. My gig is legit. I work in mall maintenance."

"Man, you're a janitor?" Maxwell teased. "I never would've guessed that. If you wanted to work in the mall, I could have easily given you a job in my store."

"Dude, cool out with all of that. All you need to worry about is that I'm getting my paper legally. I got some things brewing, and working at the airport alone wasn't going to get it done. As for working in your store, you and I both know I'm not a suit and tie type of guy."

"I hear you, man. I can't hate on you for taking care of business. I'm proud of you." Maxwell was genuinely proud of his brother. He had always admired Jason. He didn't always agree with some of the choices he made but he looked up to him, nonetheless. Having Jason work in the mall would give Maxwell the opportunity to connect with him more and to keep tabs on him.

The strained relationship between Jason and their mother made it hard to keep up with Jason because he avoided their mother as much as he could. Jason had once told Maxwell he was keeping his distance because he didn't need his little brother reporting his actions to their mother.

Jason gave Maxwell a handshake, followed by a hug. "Well, Max, I better get going. You don't have to punch a clock, but I do. I don't want the boss man to come looking for me."

"All right. I understand. Don't let me mess up your money," Maxwell joked. "Hit me up sometime this week and we can catch a bite to eat or something."

"Will do. I'll holla at you." Within minutes, Jason was completely out of sight.

Maxwell walked away smiling. Seeing his brother took his mind off of the comments his mother made earlier. Maxwell entered the store through the employee entrance at the back of the store. With limited lighting, he maneuvered his way to his office carefully. A stack of invoices stacked neatly in a bin on his desk commanded his attention. Accounts payable and payroll were top priority.

Simon was scheduled to open the store, allowing Maxwell to complete his bookkeeping uninterrupted. Maxwell keyed the final digits into the computer and uploaded the information to the payment processing center. He found it easier using a processing center rather than printing his own checks on-site. His attention to detail and careful bookkeeping helped his business to stay afloat when many of the independently owned stores were closing, due to the sluggish economy.

Maxwell interlocked his fingers, and stretched out his arms. Rotating his neck, he released the tension from his neck and shoulders. *Now that that's out of the way, I can finalize these plans,* he thought. Opening up his internet browser, he typed Ticketmaster into the search bar. Quickly, several links appeared on the screen directing him to his desired website. He scoured the site until he found the event he wanted to take Lina to for their first date. A huge smile gleamed across his face as he anticipated her reaction. Rubbing his hands together, he let out a sigh of relief. "This is going to be perfect. I'm going to blow her mind. She won't imagine this in a million years," he stated aloud. With a click of the mouse, Maxwell confirmed his purchase.

He had always considered himself a classy guy, but even Maxwell was surprised by his choice. He was determined to make sure their date would be an event Lina would never forget. Their conversation the night prior gave him the idea. She was so open and honest with him, that she made planning things with her easy. Maxwell adored Lina's transparency and desire to enjoy the life she had without reservation. She seemed to make every moment count, a quality he both admired and respected.

Secure with his decision, he pulled out his cell phone and composed a message to Lina.

Good Morning, young lady. I just wanted to drop you a quick line to let you know I'm looking forward to seeing you tomorrow night. Have a great day.

After sending the text message, Maxwell placed his phone on the desk and waited patiently for a response.

Simon tapped on the door, before letting himself in. "Hey, Max. Are you busy? I hope not, because you've got company, and I think you're gonna want to talk to this person."

Without looking up, Maxwell raised his hand and beckoned Simon to send whoever it was in.

In a sultry tone, Maxine breathed the words, "Hello, Maxwell."

Maxwell popped his head up, in surprise. "What's going on Maxine," he replied forcing a smile.

"I'm starting to think you're avoiding me. I can't seem to ever get a return call from you, and when we do make plans to go out for a bite, something always seems to come up."

Standing up behind his desk, Maxwell avoided her interrogation. "I'm sorry. It's nothing like that, honest. Hey, check this out, I need to go out to the sales floor to take care of some things, sooo...."

"No problem. I'll go with you. We can talk out there just as well as we can in here," Maxine quickly retorted. There was no way Maxwell was getting off that easily.

Surrendering, he escorted her out of his office. She trailed close behind. Once they reached the sales floor, Maxine stood back and watched Maxwell greet customers and inspect garments. He straightened racks and did anything else he could to avoid her.

Maxine was no fool. She could clearly see what he was doing, but she wasn't fazed in the least. She was going to make him her man no matter what.

"Tell you what; you promised me a raincheck, and it's almost lunch time, and I'm hungry. How about you finally make good on your word."

"Make good on what word? What you and preacher man got going on?" Jason interrupted. "Looks like I came in here just in time. It sounds like the two of you are up to something unholy."

Relieved to see Jason, Maxwell replied "Naw, man it's nothing like that. You should know me better than that. I'm real with mine. I'm not faking and shaking like some of these other cats in the pulpit."

"For your information, Jason," Maxine interrupted.

"Maxwell promised me lunch and I'm here trying to get him to make good on his promise. I see your mind is still in the gutter, just like when we were kids."

"Aw, my bad. In that case don't let me interrupt."

"Actually, I can't do lunch today. I've got way too much going on. Tell you what, why don't you and Jason go grab something. My treat," Maxwell reached into his pocket to pull out cash.

"That won't be necessary. I'm sure Jason has work he needs to do as well." Maxine stepped closer to Maxwell, making sure her perfume whiffed through his nostrils, "Since you aren't a lying man, I'm going to give you the opportunity to redeem yourself." Handing him another business card with her phone numbers on them she said. "Also, because I haven't heard from you, I assume you've lost my number. Call me when you're available."

With that being said, Maxine walked out of the store, glancing back only once to make sure he was watching her leave.

"Man, what's wrong with you?" Jason slapped Maxwell on the back.

"What are you talking about?"

Shaking his head, Jason continued. "I know you're holy and all, but does that mean you have to be crazy too? That woman, as fine as she is was all over you. She was throwing herself at you, and you acted like you didn't even notice. Man, you have lost your mind."

"No, I have not lost my mind. Just because I'm saved doesn't mean I'm less than a man. I noticed everything she did. Maxine's actions are no different from all the other women that come at me the same way. If there's one thing I can't stand, it's a woman that throws herself at a man. I can't help it. I'm just an old fashioned guy. I like to do the chasing."

Relenting, Jason looked at his younger brother with understanding. "I feel you on that. I can't get mad at you for being old fashioned. I'm just telling you if it was me, I'd be on that before she could get the J out of her mouth."

Maxwell and Jason burst into laughter, "I hear you, man, and I know you would."

Chapter 16

Lina busied herself around her apartment cleaning and re-organizing. She was determined to keep herself busy. In her mind, the busier she remained, the less time she had to focus on insignificant things. With her rotating duster in hand, she walked over to her book shelf. With intent purpose, she ran the duster thoroughly over the shelf being sure to touch every surface.

A hanging red bookmark tassel caught her attention. Placing her duster under her arm, she reached for the book it hung out of. Lina rubbed her hands over the cover and outlined the letters H-O-L-Y B-I-B-L-E with her fingers. Placing the Bible against her chest, she closed her eyes and thought of her dear grandmother, Em'mae. Em'mae had given Lina the Bible as an eighth grade graduation gift. *"Remember baby, everything you need, is found in the Word of God. As long as you keep His Word close to you, He will never lead you astray."* Grandma Em'mae's words were as fresh in her mind as the day she had spoken them.

Lina opened the Bible, revealing the location of the bookmark. Her eyes were quickly drawn to the passage highlighted with a pink marker - Jeremiah chapter twenty-nine verse eleven. She read the passage aloud. "For I know the thoughts that I think toward you, says the Lord. Thoughts of peace and not of evil, to give you a future and a hope." Closing her eyes, and nodding her head in acceptance, Lina whispered, "Thank you, Lord."

****

Lina removed her cell phone from her purse and scrolled through her messages. The constant beeping drew her attention away from her conversation with Cheri. Cheri had called and invited her to an early lunch. The timing was perfect. After the emotional night and morning she had, Cheri's invitation was a welcomed distraction.

"You are so rude. Here I am telling you all about my workplace drama and you just picked up the phone like I wasn't even talking."

"Hold on a second, girl. You know my cell phone doubles as my office phone. I'm expecting a call from the new art gallery that's opening on Stony Island." Focusing her attention back to the phone, Lina opened the message from Maxwell. An involuntary grin formed on her lips.

Cheri reached over the table, "Let me see that phone, because you're holding out on me. I know you're not grinning like that over an art gallery. That kind of smile is brought on by a man."

"Quit playing, Cheri. You're going to mess around and break my phone."

"Well," Cheri exclaimed. "Are you going to tell me, or do I have to pry it out of you?"

"It's nothing, girl. Maxwell just sent me a message saying 'good morning'. That's all."

Cheri studied Lina. She hadn't ever seen Lina react this way to a guy that was interested in her. Over the years she had witnessed several men express interest in her friend, but they were usually met with a cold shoulder. The lucky few that did have the opportunity to take Lina out were often dismissed after a couple of dates. Lina hadn't had any real boyfriends for as long as Cheri could remember.

"That huge grin on your face says you're lying. You're actually cheesing over there." Cheri noted in disbelief.

"I am not cheesing," Lina stressed. "It's not that serious. You're just reading more into it than you should. Besides, I have a lot more to smile about than a text message. Things are going really good for me right now. My business is picking up big time. I got my royalty check from one of the magazines I shoot for and it was more than I could have imagined. All I could do was say praise the Lord." Lina waved her hands in the air, laughing.

Cheri returned her laugh and shook her head. "Ooh, girl, I'm praising Him with you." Cheri waved her hands, "Thank you for blessing my friend, Lord. Thank you so much, because now she can pick up the check, Jesus. Thank you, Jesus."

"Quit playing with God, Cheri."

"I'm not playing, I'm praising for real because I'm broke like a mug."

"What's going on with you at work?" Lina was hoping to turn the attention back to Cheri and off of herself.

Cheri used dramatic gestures to express her discontent with the staff she supervised. She had only been the billing manager for Danley Finance Corporation for a few months, but she was feeling the pressure that came along with leadership.

"Can you believe the girl had the nerve to call the customer and threaten to go to the woman's job to collect? We don't that." Cheri shared story after story.

Cheri and Lina finished up their meal, chatting. As the two parted ways, Lina reassured Cheri that her friendship with Maxwell was just that, a friendship. Nothing more, nothing less.

The phone rang just as Lina arrived at her car. Looking at the Caller ID, she quickly noticed Maxwell's name. Trying to mask her excitement, she answered in her business tone. "Lina Fairweather here, how may I help you?"

"Lina, its Maxwell. How are you?"

"Oh, Maxwell, hello. I'm doing good. How about yourself?"

Relaxing into the conversation, Maxwell shared his excitement concerning their first date. "I completed our reservations earlier today. I'm looking forward to seeing you."

"So where are we going? I need to know how to dress."

"Well, I'm not telling you where we're going. It's a surprise. Dress casual; I want you to be comfortable."

"Are you serious right now? You're really not going to tell me where we're going. How am I supposed to know where to meet you?"

Maxwell struggled to hide his frustration. After all, he thought Lina had finally gotten comfortable with him. During their previous conversation, she said she would allow him to pick her up. Now she was talking about meeting him somewhere. He would never do anything to put her in a compromising position. Besides, he was a minister. Surely, that had to count for something. "I thought I would pick you up. It would certainly make things easier based on what I have planned. Please, trust me on this one, okay?"

Unable to resist the soft rumble of Maxwell's baritone voice, Lina surrendered. "Ok, you win. I'll ride with you." Lina expelled air in frustration, only to be met with Maxwell's laughter. "Will you at least tell me what time I need to be ready? I can't have you coming to my house and find me looking crazy."

"Sure, be ready around six. That'll give us plenty of time to reach our destination."

Lina recited her address to Maxwell and ended the call. She

tried to hide her excitement, but it wasn't working. She didn't know what it was but there was something about Maxwell that could get to her every time. The harder she worked on putting her guards up, the easier he seemed to find it to tear them down again. She had to constantly remind herself that a real relationship was beyond her reach. That thought alone would keep her grounded. No matter how excited she became, she knew in the back of her mind that her situation would never be accepted. Never.

Being alone was difficult at times, which is why she allowed herself to date occasionally, but she would always stop short of developing a relationship. If the guy she was dating even hinted on wanting more, she would cut all ties instantly. There was no since in prolonging the inevitable, was the excuse she used to validate her actions. Somehow, she knew she would have to be careful this time around because Maxwell had already made his persistence evident.

"What have I gotten myself into?" she muttered before grabbing her camera and stepping out of the car.

Chapter 17

Maxwell arrived at the barbershop in the midst of a heated debate about basketball. The barbershop was the place that he felt most comfortable. He didn't have to seek to impress anyone, and he knew no one would be trying to impress him. Everyone was free with their opinions. First time patrons and longtime friends alike were welcomed and pulled into the conversations.

Taking a seat in an empty barber chair, Maxwell jumped right in as if he had been there all day. "I don't care what nobody says, the Bulls are gonna take it tonight."

"Man, you crazy. The Bulls can't stand up to the Heat," a bystander yelled from the other side of the room.

Gleaming with excitement, Maxwell set up in his chair. Chiming in, he yelled, "Man, you must be out of your mind. The Bulls are coming off a five game winning streak. Plus, we're playing at home. They're not about to let nobody show them up at home. We're dominating, son."

"Yeah, until tonight. You know the Bulls can hang it up," another patron blurted out.

Laughter filled the shop. "Max, that young cat was hanging with you. You can't shake him," Louis, the shop owner, said.

"Aw, man, he don't know what he's talking about. He's still wet behind the ears. He'll see tonight."

Maxwell relaxed in the chair while Louis gave him his usual haircut and clean shave. "Make sure you hook me up. I got plans tonight, and your boy has to look good."

"I got you, man. You already know." Louis carefully lined Maxwell's edges and removed his facial stubble. Within a few moments, he was shaved, shampooed, and on his way.

After leaving the barbershop, and running a few errands, Maxwell hurried home to get ready for his evening out with Lina. Turning on the shower, he stood in the midst of the massaging spray, adjusting the temperature until steam filled the room. Streams of the heated moisture beat against his neck and shoulders, relieving the tension that had settled in his muscles. The rhythm of the water had a calming effect that allowed him to think about the evening he had planned. He liked Lina, and wanted to make a good impression on her. He hoped his plans would be on point, and not backfire. Only time would tell.

After his shower, Maxwell slid into a pair of blue jeans and a dark red polo shirt. Dark blue and gray Nike Air Max shoes completed his ensemble. Taking a final look in the mirror, he grabbed his keys and wallet and headed to his vehicle. Just as he approached the door, his telephone rang, commanding his attention. Not wanting to miss a call from Lina, he hurried over to the phone. He picked up the phone and pressed the Answer button without hesitation.

"Hello."

"Hi, Max. Did I catch you at a bad time? Sounds like you're out of breath."

Irritated, Maxwell stared at the phone. "Actually, Maxine, you did catch me at a bad time. I'm on my way out the door. Can I call you back, perhaps tomorrow?"

Maxine struggled to find words that would keep his attention. She was beginning to believe he was interested in another woman, but refusing to tell her.

"Actually, I was calling in a prayer request. My mother

went to the doctor today and received a bad report," she lied. She was desperate, and if telling a little white lie about her mother was going to get her the attention she sought, then so be it. "I've been at her house all afternoon trying to calm her down. The doctor told her they need to run some more tests before they can develop a plan of action. I know God is able to heal her, but right now I'm too upset to do anything, including praying. Will you pray for her?"

Maxwell felt bad about rushing Maxine off the phone when her mother was facing such an awful situation. "I'm so sorry to hear that. One thing is for sure, God is able to heal all manner of disease. Of course, I'll pray with you."

Maxwell offered up a short, heartfelt prayer on behalf of Maxine's mother. At the conclusion of the prayer he surprised Maxine by ending the call.

Maxine sat on the sofa fuming. She couldn't believe he would rush off the phone after receiving such devastating news, even if it was a lie. *And he's supposed to be a preacher,* she thought. It was time for her to do some major investigative work. Something was up and she was going to find out what or who it was.

Pulling out of the garage, Maxwell felt bad about cutting Maxine short. He wondered if he had gotten so caught up in impressing Lina that he lost sight of his ministerial duties. Within a matter of minutes, he had convinced himself that he was ok. He had prayed just as she had asked. He also asked her to keep him posted on her mother's condition. There really wasn't much more he could have done.

Glancing at the clock, he read the numbers five thirty-five aloud. According to the directions Lina had given him, he figured he was at least thirty minutes away from her apartment. Heading East on 87th Street, Maxwell turned left onto Western

Avenue. Every light on Western seemed to turn red just as he approached them. He continued on Western until he reached Mountain Avenue. Turning onto Mountain Avenue he arrived at Lina's apartment with minutes to spare.

He let down his sun visor for a quick, final look before seeing Lina. He hoped she would be ready. He didn't want to sit around very long waiting. Walking up the steps to her apartment, he took slow rhythmic breaths. By the time he reached the top he was relaxed and ready for his date. Pressing the lighted doorbell button he heard bell chimes coming from inside. To his surprise, she quickly appeared at the door. Pushing him back out of the way, she locked her door and turned to him.

"Hello," he said, still dazed at her quick actions.

"I'm rude, huh?" she laughed. "Hello, Maxwell."

Studying her appearance, Maxwell smiled. Long, flowing curls rested on her shoulders above a royal blue and white peasant style shirt. Dark blue denim jeans and royal blue and white ballet style flats completed her look. Bangle bracelets lined her right arm, alternating in color from royal blue to white. Finally, thin, white hoop earrings completed her ensemble.

"You look very nice," he complimented, as he opened the door for her.

"Thanks, you too," was her quick response. She couldn't let him see the delight in her eyes at his appearance. Her heart rate seemed to increase when her eyes rested on the muscles bulging from his short-sleeved shirt.

The scent of his cologne filled the vehicle, tantalizing her senses. Lina decided to initiate small talk in order to help her to regain focus. "Okay, Maxwell, I'm in your vehicle now, so can you please enlighten me on your plans for the evening."

Maxwell displayed a sheepish grin as he pulled away from the curb. "You'll just have to see."

Although Lina was curious about their destination she remained calm. The element of surprise had her giddy with excitement.

****

Maxwell pulled the car into the closest available parking lot. He didn't want Lina to have to walk too far.

Lina observed the bright lights and signs outside of the United Center. When her eyes fell on the statue of Michael Jordan she shrieked, "Oh my God, Maxwell. You got us tickets to the Bulls game. Wow." Shock and amazement displayed on her face. She tried to play it cool, but the thought of seeing her first professional basketball game excited her. "I've always wanted to do this. I don't know why I haven't before now."

Maxwell matched her smile with one of his own. "You know what? None of that matters." He paused. "We're here now. Let's find the Will Call window. I need to pick up our tickets."

Perfectly in tune, Maxwell and Lina walked over to the window and retrieved their tickets. Once inside the United Center, they walked past the concession area. He offered to buy her some refreshments, but Lina graciously declined. She couldn't wait to get inside. As suave as Maxwell was she figured he had purchased courtside seats. Lina took the lead, hurrying into the arena. She went into the door that led to the floor seats.

Maxwell laughed under his breath. "Uh, Lina."

"Yeah," she replied with a full grin.

"Our seats are up there," he said, pointing to an area higher up than where they stood. He struggled to keep from laughing aloud. Her facial expression was one of disbelief.

"Are you sure?" she asked. She wasn't trying to seem unappreciative. She just expected something totally different from him.

"I'm sure." Extending the tickets to her, he pointed out the seat numbers. "See, it's right here. Section 233, seats nine and ten. We can take the elevator if you prefer."

"That's okay; I don't mind taking the stairs." Lina followed Maxwell up the stairs to their section. *I guess that's what I get for assuming.*

The game was everything Maxwell had hoped it would be. Although their seats were fairly high up, they still had a good view of the game. Best of all, the Bulls didn't disappoint their fans. They were clearly on top of their game, ending with a twelve point lead over the Miami Heat.

Lina blended in with the crowd perfectly. Cheering for the Bulls and yelling at the opposing team whenever they fouled her beloved Derrick Rose. Maxwell glanced at her several times throughout the game. He was amused by how focused she was. He couldn't remember the last time he had enjoyed a basketball game as much as he did being with Lina.

After the game was over, they were both noticeably hungry. They returned to Maxwell's vehicle. Once inside, he started the truck. The engine hummed gently. "I made reservations for us at Jimmy's on the park, but if you prefer something else I'll be happy to oblige."

"I'm happy you said that because I'm in the mood for pizza," she said. "In fact, I know the perfect place."

"Pizza sounds good, just tell me where and we'll head that way."

"Let's go to Home Run Inn Pizza on 31st." Lina's enthusiasm displayed in her tone. "I have loved their pizza since the first time I tried it. Cheri took me there for lunch one day and I have been hooked ever since."

Maxwell looked at her puzzled. "I keep forgetting you're

not from here. I've been eating their pizzas since I was a kid."
Hoping to not sound condescending he added, "You're right
though, their pizza is some of the best around."

The twenty minute ride gave Maxwell and Lina the
opportunity to talk about a variety of subjects, including their
childhood. He could tell she was growing more and more
comfortable with him. Lina relaxed in her seat and crossed her
legs. They talked about the expectations she felt her parents
held for her. Having siblings that were academically inclined,
in her opinion, delivered added pressure for her to excel
academically. Lina folded her hands in her lap as she spoke.

Thinking she had totally released her guard, Maxwell took
the opportunity to place his hand on top of hers.

Snatching her hand back quickly, she yelled, "What do you
think you're doing? Are you crazy?"

Startled by her instant displeasure, Maxwell stuttered
an apology, "I'm, I'm so sorry. I didn't mean to make you
uncomfortable. I promise I wasn't trying to do anything to you.
I just felt so comfortable with you; I thought it would be okay.
I'm sorry. I promise it won't happen again."

Maxwell spoke so rapidly that Lina couldn't help but laugh.
She couldn't stay mad after seeing how bad she had scared the
poor man.

Totally confused, he looked at Lina as if she had lost her
mind. "Do you have a split personality or something?" he
asked sincerely. "I'm just saying, one minute you're yelling to
the top of your lungs, and the next minute you're cracking up
laughing." He didn't mean to speak so bluntly, but Lina had
struck a nerve.

She laughed harder. "No, I don't have a split personality. I
was upset for real. Then you started talking so fast when you
were apologizing that it sounded like you were speaking in

tongues. I couldn't help but laugh."

"Well, I know one thing; I won't touch your hand again. I'm just going to keep my hands on the wheel where they're safe." Lina continued to laugh. "That's right. Keep your hands to yourself."

Chapter 18

"Oh, my God." Lina exclaimed. "Girl, I had a great time." Lina's excitement reverberated through the phone.

Cheri couldn't help but be excited for her friend. She had never received a call like this from Lina. It was usually the other way around with Cheri sharing one of her exploits with Lina. Whatever Maxwell had done clearly worked because this was not the Lina that she knew.

"Don't leave me in suspense. Tell me everything. I want details."

"If you want details then you better get comfortable, because I have a lot to tell you." Lina kicked her shoes off and sat on the side of her bed. She felt like a giddy school girl coming home from her first date.

"Okay, so first of all, he came and picked me up. As soon as he rung my door bell, I darted out the door. Then,"

"Hold up," Cheri interrupted. "You didn't let him in?"

"Nope," Lina confirmed.

"And you answered the door on the first ring? Lord, have mercy. You are so out of touch. I have a lot to teach you," Cheri said.

"Forget you," Lina laughed, "I got this. I wasn't about to let him inside my apartment. I don't know him like that. Shoot, getting my address was a major accomplishment for him because I don't roll like that either."

"I don't know what I'm going to do with you."

"Love me. That's about all you can do."

"I know that's right," Cheri replied.

"Now if you're done with your commercial break, I'll tell you the rest."

"Go ahead, I want to hear this."

Lina paused for a moment, making sure she kept things in order. "Where was I? Oh yeah, so he picked me up and he was looking good as usual."

"Was he dressed up?"

"No, he just had on blue jeans and a dark red polo shirt. I could tell he had a fresh haircut and he was clean shaven. I'm telling you, the brother was fine. Plus, he had that Escalade shining too."

"What did you wear?" Cheri's excitement matched Lina's.

Lina put her feet up on the bed as she continued her conversation with her best friend. "I wore my royal blue and white peasant blouse with those dark blue jeans I got when we went shopping last week. And, I had on my royal blue and white flats. Oh yeah, I flat ironed my hair, and put a few curls in it."

"I can't believe you straightened your hair. You never wear your hair straightened. I'll bet you were so pretty. Girl, what did he say when he saw you?"

"Before or after he looked me up and down," she boasted. "For real though, he was like, 'you look really nice, Lina'. I was trying my best to keep from grinning."

Cheri adjusted herself on her couch. She felt like she was watching a romantic movie. "Okay, okay so you get in the car and go where." Cheri was becoming anxious.

Lina could tell the suspense was about to get the best of Cheri. "If you stop interrupting me I can tell you everything."

"All right, I won't interrupt any more. Go ahead." Cheri

relented.

"At first he wouldn't tell me where we were going. That part just about drove me crazy because you know how I am about surprises."

"Um hmm," was all Cheri muttered. She was not about to let Lina stop again.

Continuing, Lina said, "When we finally arrived we were at the United Center. Girl, he took me to see the Bulls play the Miami Heat."

"He took you to a basketball game?" Cheri interrupted. "Girl, I thought you were about to say he really did something special."

"Cheri, you are so rude. Plus, you're missing the point." Lina quickly became agitated with Cheri.

"I'm sorry, what's the point that I missed?"

Rolling her eyes, Lina's tone displayed her irritation. "The point is," she stressed, "he actually listened to me when we talked on the phone. I told him I had never been to a professional basketball game, and that I really wanted to go one day."

"Girl, you haven't ever been to a Bulls game? My bad, I thought the brother was taking you to do something he wanted to do. I didn't realize it was that deep."

"Do you want me to finish telling you about our date or not?"

"Yeah, go ahead."

"Anyway, when we got there I went strutting towards the courtside seats and he was like 'our seats are up there' pointing all the way up. Girl, I was so embarrassed."

Cheri burst into laughter. "Dang, girl. I know you were embarrassed. I'll bet that was some funny stuff." Cheri laughed harder, "Man, I wish I could have seen that."

"It was pretty funny." Lina joined Cheri in laughter. "I thought he was going to go all out of his way to impress me, but I'm glad things turned out the way that did. I feel like I got a chance to see the real Maxwell."

"Where did he take you to eat? I know he fed you afterwards."

"He had made reservations at Jimmy's on the park, but ultimately he left the dinner choice up to me, and I wanted pizza, so you know where we went."

"Home Run Inn," the ladies said in unison.

"During dinner we talked about all kinds of stuff. Everything from how our day had been before our date to our favorite television shows as children."

"Did he kiss you?" Cheri asked, eager for Lina's answer.

"No, he did not kiss me," Lina retorted, "He tried to hold my hand but I snatched it back from him. I'm not ready for all of that. After dinner he brought me home, walked me to my door, I shook his hand, and thanked him for a lovely evening, and that was that on that."

"Wow, girl, this sounds like something I would read in those romance novels I like."

"I don't know about that. I just know I had a wonderful evening, and I'm looking forward to next time, if there is a next time."

"There'll be a next time. It sounds like he really likes you."

"Hold on, Cheri, I've got a beep." Lina removed the phone from her ear and looked at the display. "Girl, it's him. Hold on, okay."

Lina pushed the button to accept the incoming call. "Hello," she answered cheerfully.

"Hello, Lina." Maxwell's smooth baritone voice oozed through the phone line. "I just arrived home. I wanted to let you know I had a great time with you this evening. I hope we can do it again sometime soon."

"I had a good time also." Lina maintained a calm exterior, but her insides were all over the place. "I'd enjoy going out with you again."

"Okay, cool," Maxwell smiled. "I better let you go. It's getting pretty late."

Lina ended the call with Maxwell and resumed her call with Cheri. "I'm sorry, girl. I thought you had hung up."

"And miss out on hearing about what he had to say. I don't think so."

Laughing, Lina filled Cheri in on her brief conversation with Maxwell. After making sure Cheri was thoroughly briefed, Lina ended her call. She was completely exhausted.

After a quick shower and pinning her hair up, Lina lay quietly in the bed. She smiled as she reflected on the night's events. Maxwell was wearing her down and she knew it. He seemed so genuine in his approach, and he wasn't pushing her. No matter how hard she tried, she was finding it harder and harder to keep him from penetrating her heart. Lina replayed the evening in her mind until she was overtaken by sleep.

Chapter 19

"Hi Maxwell, This is Maxine. I'm sorry to keep calling, but I wanted to give you an update on my mother's condition. Give me a call when you get a chance, ok. Thank you, buh-bye." Maxine's voice was sultry. She was hoping her message would trigger concern in Maxwell, prompting him to return her call.

Standing in the mirror, she smoothed her sleek lengthy tresses. Her eight hundred dollar weave job was worth every penny in her opinion. Only the best would do, for her. As long as she kept her body tight and her game on point, she would always have the best and never have to pay a dime for it. Her sugar daddy would definitely make sure of that.

After obtaining her position as a paralegal at Freeman, Reynolds, and associates it wasn't hard for her to make herself known to the founding partner Jonathan Freeman. The fact that he was married was a mere technicality. He wasn't the first married man she had successfully conquered, so she knew what it would take to make him come around.

Their ongoing affair afforded her the opportunity to take exotic vacations, drive expensive vehicles, dine at the best restaurants, stay at five star hotels all over the world, and wear the absolute best in designer clothing. Maxine had no plans to give any of her luxuries up. She would just have to find a way to fit both her current lifestyle and a relationship with Maxwell into her perfectly planned out puzzle.

Smoothing on glossy lipstick, she took a final glance before grabbing her Chanel handbag and heading out the door. Maxine entered the secure parking lot of her downtown high rise apartment building, and made her way to her pearl white Maserati GranCabrio. Pressing the unlock button on her key fob she slid into the driver's seat. She turned the key and listened to the roar of the engine. With the press of a button she selected her favorite satellite radio station and pulled out.

The whole chasing Maxwell thing was getting old to her. She hadn't had a man to resist her since she was in Junior High School when she wore braces and pigtails. The only explanation she could come up with was there had to be another woman. Even if that was the case it didn't make sense. Maxine didn't take rejection well and she was determined to do whatever it took to make Maxwell hers. For now, Maxwell had to be put on the back burner. She had other obligations to meet.

****

Without looking, Maxwell reached into his pocket and silenced his cell phone. It had been ringing constantly all morning long. He had assigned individual ringtones to both his mother and Lina so he knew neither of the calls were coming from them. Whoever it was would just have to wait. He had promised Pastor James that he would get some estimates on the parking lot expansion for the church. At the moment, that was his main priority. Simon was running the store so that Maxwell could work undisturbed.

Several phone calls later, his task was complete. He had successfully scheduled five appointments with contractors. He made a brief call to Pastor James outlining the details of his research. Finally, he was ready to shift his attention to other things. His phone beeped loudly, notifying him of waiting voicemail messages. Maxwell hesitantly removed his cell phone from his pocket. He pressed the appropriate key to retrieve his messages. Pulling the phone away from his ear, he stared in disbelief. Maxine had left him a message concerning her mother that carried a seductive tone. He didn't want to read too much into it, but something didn't seem right. She sounded more like a woman seeking a date than a concerned child requesting prayer.

"Maybe I'm wrong," he exclaimed out loud. "Lord, I don't want to accuse her of anything, but I've been here before and it's way too familiar." He inhaled deeply and dropped his head in surrender.

Determined to do the right thing, he picked his phone up and dialed Maxine's phone number. Several rings later, her voicemail greeting played in his ear, "Hey, Maxine, this is Maxwell. I was calling in response to your message. I have been pretty tied up this morning. I pray all is well with your mother and your family as a whole. We'll talk later."

Relief swept through Maxwell like a welcomed breeze. He had done his part by returning her call and showing his concern. Before returning to the sales floor, he decided to make one final phone call. Placing his feet on top of the desk, he leaned back in his chair and quickly selected the phone number from his list of contacts.

The moment the call was connected his mood changed. His humdrum demeanor was replaced by enthusiasm. "Good morning, Miss Fairweather. How are you doing?"

Lina met Maxwell's enthusiasm with excitement of her own. "Hi, Maxwell. I'm doing great. How about yourself?"

"Much better now." Maxwell's smile could be heard in his voice. "I've been working all morning, taking care of church business. Now that I've finished, I thought I'd give you a call to see what you were up to."

"I'm doing some editing, but I can definitely use a break."

Lina got up from her desk and plopped down on the sofa.

"I didn't mean to interrupt your artistic flow," he teased. "I know you got skills. I checked you out."

"What? How?" Lina exclaimed. She was surprised at Maxwell's comment.

"I'm serious," he replied chuckling. When we had lunch downtown, you revealed your profession to me, so I decided to check it out."

"You mean check me out. Did you think I was lying or something?" Lina's words were accusatory.

"Calm down. It was nothing like that. I just wanted to see your work. At that point I didn't know when I would get an opportunity to sit down with you again. I had a little extra time one day. That's when I looked you up online and found out the names and locations of the galleries here in Chicago where your work is on display."

Lina softened at Maxwell's words. She liked the fact that he was interested not only in her, but also in her work. "Stalker," she jested.

"I am not a stalker," he shot back. "Let's just say, I'm a connoisseur of beautiful things."

"Oh, really." Lina laughed abruptly into the phone. "You can give it whatever fancy name you want, but we common folk like to call it stalking."

"No, you didn't just go there." Maxwell matched her laughter. One thing he had come to know about Lina was she always seemed to lighten his mood. The connection they had was incomparable to his previous relationships. She didn't put on a front like most of the women he dated. She was unique, and he admired that about her. Bringing the conversation back to its main purpose, he changed subjects.

"I had a good time with you the other night. I can't wait to see you again. What are you doing this weekend? I'd like to take you out."

"I'm shooting a wedding this Saturday. I'm not sure how long that's going to take, so I really can't say for sure."

"What about Friday night?" Maxwell was persistent.

"This wedding is a pretty big deal, so I'll be spending Friday night preparing."

"Are you taking pictures of celebrities or something? Or are they just a bunch of rich people." Maxwell tried to mask his disappointment.

"No, I'm not shooting celebrities or rich people." Lina paused for a moment and pondered a thought. "You know what. The couple did say I was welcome to bring a guest with me. This is highly unusual, and not the way I normally operate, but I could use an assistant and Cheri is going to be busy this weekend. Why don't you tag along?"

"Really? Are you sure I won't be in your way. I don't know the first thing about photography. I don't want to mess up and tarnish your reputation."

"I'm sure. As a matter of fact, I'll use your muscles to carry everything. Surely you can't mess that up," she joked. It's a formal wedding so I need you to wear a suit."

"Look at you. Already telling me how to dress and we're not even married yet."

Lina was taken aback by Maxwell's response. "Slow your roll, cowboy. It ain't that kind of party."

Maxwell laughed at the seriousness of Lina's tone. One thing about her, she could go from cracking up laughing to courthouse serious in a millisecond. "I'm just messing with you, girl. What time should I come by?"

"I'll give you the details later. Right now I have to get back to work, and you should do the same, mister minister, slash entrepreneur, slash pain in my neck."

"Oh, I see you got jokes. That's okay. I'll get you back for that one. Right now I really do have work I should probably be doing. We'll touch base later."

"I'm sure we will, Mr. Lee. Bye, bye now."

"All right, take care of yourself and have a good rest of the day." Maxwell ended his call with a smile.

Chapter 20

Lina ended her call with Maxwell and quickly dialed Cheri's work number. Cheri picked up on the first ring with her usual greeting.

"Guess who just called me," Lina yelled into the phone.

Cheri was surprised at Lina's zeal. "I don't know. Who?"

"Really, Cheri. You're seriously going to act like you don't know?"

"Are you talking about Maxwell?" Cheri inquired

"Who else would I be talking about? Quit playing."

"I didn't know. I wasn't there. For all I know you could've been talking about Jim Bob the plumber." Cheri giggled softly into the phone.

"You make me so sick, with your silly self. By the way, Steve Harvey called; he said get off the stage because you're not funny."

Continuing to laugh, Cheri said, "You're just mad I got your butt. Don't act like you don't want to laugh."

"Whatever. I'm not laughing at your silly behind."

Cheri's position as the office manager gave her the freedom to take a moment to talk with her friend. "So what did you and Maxwell talk about?" Cheri placed extra emphasis on Maxwell's name.

"Not a whole lot. He asked me to go out with him this weekend. I told him I couldn't make it. Then I invited him to a wedding. He accepted. End of story."

"Hold up. Don't be trying to speed through all of that. Did I just hear you say you invited him to a wedding? You're getting in a little deep aren't you, girlfriend."

"It's not like that. I need an assistant. You've got plans, and can't go with me. He was available, so I asked him. End of story."

"Just that simple, huh?" Cheri replied sarcastically.

"Yep; just that simple."

"Don't even try it, Lina. You really like this guy. I can hear it all in your voice."

"Let's just say he's growing on me, but don't worry. I'm taking things slow. I know what I'm doing."

"I hope you're right. A wedding is a very intimate setting. I just don't want you to get hurt, and I don't want him to get the wrong idea." Cheri's concern was evident.

"Girl, calm down. I got this. You're reading way too much into it. I promise you, I'm good."

"Ok, I believe you. You know I'm not used to this because in the two years I've known you, I've never seen you act like this over any guy."

"Maxwell and I are just friends Cheri, dang." Lina was starting to regret her call to Cheri. She didn't want to have to keep explaining herself. After all she didn't look at Maxwell in that way. Or did she?

Cheri relented. "I'm sorry, my bad. I'm just looking out for my girl."

"I know, and I'm sorry too. I completely overreacted. I better let you get back to work."

"Yeah, I better go. Tell you what, I'll come over this evening, and we can hang out. We need some girl time, anyway. Besides, I know you don't have a clue about what to wear to the wedding."

"That's a great idea," Lina agreed. Since you're coming over, I better grab something out of the freezer. I'll whip us up a little something."

"Cool, and I'll pick up a movie on my way over," Cheri offered, before disconnecting the call.

Lina looked over at the screen saver displaying various photos. "Whelp, back to work."

****

Working was almost pointless. Lina was far too distracted. With frustration, she rose from her desk and went into the kitchen. Filling a sport's bottle with cold water, she decided to take a walk. She quickly went into her bedroom and slipped on her favorite pair of athletic shoes. Hopefully the fresh air would help to clear her mind.

Why does life have to be so complicated? she thought. She had successfully avoided getting involved with men who were interested in long term relationships up to this point. Now here was Maxwell, a handsome, successful man who could have his pick from droves of women. However, he seemed bound and determined to become a part of her life. Although Maxwell jokingly made the remark they weren't married yet, and she was already telling him how to dress, Lina couldn't help but to take the statement to heart. Marriage was not something that was available to her, and she couldn't allow her mind to imagine otherwise.

Lina looked around in surprise. She had walked three miles without realizing it. There were times like these that she wished she still lived in Durham. Although her mother was over the top at times, she was compassionate and she would know just the right things to say. Calling her mother right now would be a bad idea. The heavy breathing that resulted from her brisk walk would send Lydia into an instant panic. She most certainly would assume the worst. Thoughts of her mother put a smile on Lina's face. Following a brief stretch, Lina headed back to her apartment. She purposed within herself to relax and to live in the moment. No sense in stressing prematurely. She and Maxwell were becoming good friends and she was determined to leave it at that.

Lina returned to her apartment feeling rejuvenated. She peeled her sweaty clothes off and entered the shower. The intense flow of water from the shower was just what Lina needed. Moving her head from side to side, she allowed the massaging water to ease the tension that had settled into her tired muscles. Leaning her head back, she allowed the water to penetrate her thick curls until it reached her scalp. On the trek back home, she had allowed herself to release the tension that threatened to overtake her.

She couldn't afford to burden herself down with a bunch of what ifs. Life was a daily process. She wasn't going to miss out on not one moment of the pleasures the present held. Gone was yesterday, and tomorrow was uncertain. She had purposed within herself to live a life without regrets. To put it simply, if what she was planning to do was going to lead to regrets, she basically wouldn't do it. She had been told on numerous occasions by Cheri and others that she shared her philosophy with that it was ridiculous. Lina didn't care. She felt life was all about choices and she chose to remain confident and to keep a positive outlook.

Lina completed her shower feeling refreshed. Time was quickly passing. She stepped into her bedroom, and selected a Duke University t-shirt and a matching pair of lounge pants with Duke printed down the side. After pulling her hair into a ponytail, she returned to her photo editing. She attacked the task with fervor. Much to her delight, she successfully completed her task within a few hours.

Cheri sent Lina a text message letting her know she would be there in an hour. Lina decided to go ahead and start dinner. Her menu included meatloaf, corn on the cob and fresh green beans. Iced tea chilled in the refrigerator completing her meal.

Thoughts of her parents remained fresh on her mind as she cooked. It had been more than a week since she had last spoken with them. After putting the meatloaf in the oven, she decided to give her mother a call.

Lydia picked up the call almost immediately. "Hey, baby girl."

"Hey, Mama," Lina replied gleefully. "How's everybody doing?"

"We're all doing fine, baby. How are things going with you?"

Lina could hear the sound of pots rattling in the background. She figured her mother was cooking. Lydia was always trying some new recipe and using her husband as her personal taste tester. "I'm doing good," she replied. "Staying extremely busy as usual, but God knows I can't complain. My demand has more than doubled so I don't have a lot of idle time."

"That's a blessing, baby girl. You always have been real good at taking pictures. Zarion loved the pictures you took of her when you were here. She has already put them in her baby book. It won't be long before the little man is here."

The thought of being an aunt excited Lina. She could hardly wait for the baby to make his arrival. She was prepared to spend several weeks in Durham following his birth. "I can't wait until he's born. I'm going to take so many pictures of him. I've already ordered a photo album with his name embroidered across the front."

"Zarion will love that." Lydia continued to rattle pots in the background. "That's enough about us. How are you doing? Are you taking care of yourself?"

"Yes, Mama, I'm taking care of myself." Lina quickly changed the subject. She didn't want her mother to start drilling her. "Did I mention I went to a Bulls game last week when I talked to you?"

"Did you? Honey, that's great. I'm glad to hear you're getting out more. Did Cheri go with you?"

"No, I went with a guy named Maxwell. He and Cheri attend the same church. He's a minister."

"Oh, I see." Lydia's tone was bland. "Did you have a good time?" she asked.

"Mama, it's not even like that. We're just friends. I'm not trying to go there with him, or any man for that matter."

"Well, baby, I'm glad you have a friend. It's nice to have a male companion. You're a young woman. You should be able to enjoy a man's company. You're a responsible woman. You know how far to go."

"How's Daddy doing? I haven't talked to him in a while."

"He's right here. Hold on a minute, and I'll get him."

Lina could hear her mother passing the phone over to her father.

"Hey, baby. How's my princess?"

"I'm doing great, Daddy. I miss you and mama." Lina felt like a little girl talking to her father. She had always been a daddy's girl. Being the youngest among her siblings she was the most spoiled. "Well, baby. We miss you too. You know I don't like you being in that big ole city by yourself." Mr. Fairweather's voice was deep and scratchy.

"I know you don't, but you raised me right. I can take care of myself." Lina displayed confidence in her tone. "You don't have to worry about me. More than anything, you know God has my back."

"You said something there, girl. Your mama and I keep you lifted up in prayer. One thing about the God I serve, He is faithful, baby."

"Amen, Daddy."

Never being the one to hold a long conversation, Mr. Fairweather stopped abruptly. "Okay, baby. I'm gonna give you back to your mother. I'll check with you later."

"All right, Daddy. I love you, and I'll talk to you soon."

"You know he's not going to hold a long conversation," Lydia laughed. "That man is going to make it short, sweet, and to the point, every time."

"I know that's right," Lina agreed. "Now, I'm going to follow his lead. Cheri is coming over. We're going to eat and watch a chick flick. I love y'all, and I'm so glad to hear your voice."

"We love you too, baby. Take care of yourself and don't forget to pray."

"Yes, Mama. I will. Tell everybody I said, hello." Lina made a kissing sound into the phone and disconnected the call. She was glad to know her family was doing well. It was hard being so far away from home, but she was building a life for herself in Chicago and she had no room for regrets.

****

Cheri rang the doorbell and waited for Lina to answer. With a big smile on her face, she extended her arms, revealing the gift she brought Lina. "Truce?" she asked, when Lina opened the door.

"You're not fighting fair. You know I can't resist Garrett's popcorn." She grabbed the small tin container and stepped aside for Cheri to enter.

"Umm, something smells good," Cheri complimented. "What all did you cook?"

"It's just meatloaf and some veggies. Put your stuff down so we can eat. I'm starved."

Cheri quickly complied. The ladies fixed their plates and took a seat on the couch in front of the television. Cheri got up and placed the movie in the DVD player.

"I rented Love and Basketball," she said as she took a seat next to Lina.

"That is one of my all time favorite movies." Lina pressed the button on the remote control to start the movie.

While watching the movie the ladies sang along to familiar songs, and cheered the lead characters on. They had both watched the movie several times before.

"Girl, that one on one game gets to me every time." Lina declared.

"I know right. When she tells him she wants to play for his heart, I be crying like a baby."

"Yeah, I did hear you sniffling over there," Lina joked.

"Forget you, Lina."

The friends laughed easily.

Following the movie, Cheri insisted Lina allow her to help her pick out an outfit for the wedding. Once she was satisfied with the final ensemble she ended her visit.

"Lina girl, I need to get out of here. My flight leaves at eight in the morning, and I still haven't packed yet. I know you'll be working but try to have fun Saturday, ok." Cheri hugged her friend and headed for the door. "Maxwell is not going to know what hit him. Make sure you call me afterwards and give me the full play by play."

"Don't I always," Lina replied with a smirk. "I'm sure I'll be drop dead gorgeous with this big camera around my neck."

"Girl, you're silly. It's not like you'll be wearing the camera the entire time. Lighten up and enjoy the moment.

Chapter 21

Maxwell selected a black suit, with a maroon silk shirt. His necktie was black with maroon and white accents. Solid black dress shoes completed his ensemble. Walking over to his dresser, he picked up a gold, diamond cut, link chain and gold pinky ring with diamond accents. He still couldn't believe Lina had invited him to attend a wedding with her.

After much debate he had finally convinced her to allow him to drive them to the ceremony. She could be so stubborn at times. He made sure his vehicle was detailed to perfection. After ensuring he had enough room in the back for her equipment to lay unobstructed, Maxwell made his way to Lina's house.

He arrived at her apartment with plenty of time to spare before Lina was scheduled to meet with the bride. She hadn't told him much about the couple so he felt a bit awkward, but he could handle it. His career choices put him in a position where he was always meeting new people. This would be no different from welcoming visitors and new members to the church, or greeting new customers at his store.

Maxwell rang the doorbell and stood back. The last time he picked Lina up at her apartment she almost knocked him down. This time he was better prepared. The door flew open and Lina beckoned him inside.

"Hi, come on in," Lina said, almost breathless. "I need a little help. Would you mind grabbing that box by the couch?" She asked without looking up.

"Uh, sure. No problem." Maxwell moved quickly in the

direction of the box. "Is this all you need me to get?"

"Yeah, everything is pretty much in there." Lina struggled with a box of her own. "I need to grab my keys and then we can go."

"Lina, let me get that box for you. Give me just a second. I'll go and put this one in the truck, and then I'll come back for that one." There was no way Maxwell was going to watch Lina struggle to carry the box when he was more than capable of carrying it for her. "Sit it down, and grab your keys and whatever else you need. I'll be right back."

"Okay," was the only response Lina could give. She had become quite independent since moving to Chicago. Being her parents youngest child came with perks that were not available to her in Chicago. She stood back and watched as Maxwell carefully placed the boxes in the cargo area. Once the final box was loaded, she grabbed her purse and keys off the table near the door and joined him.

Lina made herself comfortable in the truck and adjusted her seatbelt. She gave Maxwell the venue address and relaxed. *I could get used to this*, she thought. Looking over at Maxwell she said, "You make a pretty good assistant. I appreciate you handling those boxes for me. Not that I couldn't do it."

"I'm sure you could have, but I didn't mind helping. After all, that's why I'm here, right?"

"Yeah, I guess you're right," she agreed, expelling a soft giggle.

When they arrived at the wedding venue, a young woman directed them to the ceremony space so that Lina could set up. Lina introduced herself to the wedding party and gave them instructions before requesting to see the bride.

Speaking directly to Maxwell, she asked, "Could you please finish unloading the equipment for me. I'm going to go and get a few shots of the bride before I take group shots of the wedding party."

"I'm on it, boss," he joked. "I'll have it in here when you return."

Lina snickered. "Quit playing, Maxwell." She rolled her eyes playfully before leaving the room to meet Victoria.

One of the hostesses escorted Lina down a long hall before arriving at the dressing room where Victoria was busy being prepped by make-up artist, hairstylist, and her wedding coordinator. Victoria turned and smiled when Lina entered the room.

"Miss Fairweather, you made it. Oh thank you so much." Victoria rose and greeted Lina with a hug."

Lina noticed there were no mirrors in the room. "Hello, Victoria. Please call me Lina." Lina returned her hug. "Everything is decorated so beautifully. This is going to be a wonderful ceremony. I'm honored that you asked me to capture this moment for you."

"I wouldn't have it any other way. I knew you were the right person for the job the moment I saw your photos hanging in the gallery."

"Thanks, Victoria, that means a lot." Lina held up her camera. "Now, the first thing I want to get is pictures of you getting ready. I'm going to stand over here out of the way and take some random shots."

Lina did a final inspection on her camera and settled on the other side of the room. Within seconds, sounds of the shutter and bright flashes filled the room. She took pictures of the hairstylist placing hair pins in Victoria's hair. The makeup artist placed eye shadow on her remaining eye. With a feather light touch, she dusted powder over her face, being careful not to draw any further attention to her missing eye. To complete

Victoria's look, she applied a few brush strokes of blush to her cheeks and smoothed gloss to her mangled lips. Lina snapped multiple pictures of the process.

Victoria stood with the support of her cane while her mother zipped the back of her gown. Her crystal and pearl beaded gown glistened under the flash of the camera. The hairstylist then stepped in and placed the veil on her head. Victoria's mother gave her a final kiss before handing her the bouquet of peach and ivory roses. Lina moved in closer to capture pictures of Victoria's completed look.

"Victoria, you look beautiful," Lina said as she struggled to hold back tears. Knowing that Jeremy continued to love Victoria in spite of her imperfections was overwhelming. *If only she could be loved that completely,* she thought. "If you'll excuse me, I need to get some pictures of the wedding party." Lina exited the room and walked swiftly down the hall until she reached the ceremony space. *I can't lose it in here,* she thought. As she requested, Maxwell had brought everything in. He had even set her tripod up in the center aisle. "Thank you," she whispered.

Maxwell nodded his head as he mouthed the words, "You're welcome." He looked on as Lina skillfully arranged the wedding party and set up various poses for them. He enjoyed watching her in her element. He didn't know why, but he sensed a hint of sadness in her eyes. She tried hard to mask it, but he could tell it was there. Not wanting to dwell on it, he surmised it as a common thing among single women at weddings.

Lina completed her pre-wedding photos, removed her tripod from the aisle, and took a seat next to Maxwell. The ceremony was scheduled to start in a half hour, so she welcomed the quick break. "Thanks for setting up the tripod. You're shaping up to be a pretty good assistant, Maxwell."

"Is that so," he replied with a questioning glance.

"Don't look at me like that." Lina reached up and covered Maxwell's eyes with her hand.

"Oh, I'm looking," he quipped. "As a matter of fact, I haven't told you how beautiful you are. That dress looks nice on you." He liked the way the knee length, lavender dress accented her subtle curves without too much exposure.

Blushing, Lina replied "Thank you."

Guests slowly began filing into the room. "I guess that's my queue. I need to get some pictures of the guests arriving. The coordinator said you can sit here during the ceremony."

"Thanks," Maxwell uttered.

The officiant, groom, and best man took their places at the front. Soft music played as the bridal party made their entrance. Maxwell watched as Lina captured every aspect on film. Two small girls rang bells, signifying the entrance of the bride. The wedding guests rose to their feet as the double doors at the back of the room opened. Maxwell pulled his lips into a tight smile. Both compassion and confusion swept through his mind. He was in no way prepared for what he saw. His smile grew with each step he saw Victoria struggle to take. She held on tightly to her father's arm as he escorted her down the short aisle. The groom displayed a smile full of love that reflected on his entire face as he watched his bride come towards him. The bride met his smile with one of her own. Lina continued to snap pictures, being careful not to interrupt the flow of the ceremony.

Jeremy stepped up to meet Victoria. Facing one another, they listened intently to the officiant. "Before Jeremy and Victoria make their vows to one another, Victoria has something special she would like to share with Jeremy," he said. Handing her the microphone he allowed her to speak freely.

In the midst of tears, Victoria looked into Jeremy's eyes

and began to speak. First Corinthians chapter thirteen verses four through eight read, *Love is patient, love is kind, it does not envy, it does not boast, it is not proud, it does not dishonor others, it is not self-seeking, it is not easily angered, it keeps no record of wrongs. Love does not delight in evil but rejoices with the truth. It always protects, always trusts, always hopes, always perseveres. Love never fails.* Tears began to fall from her eye. "I have heard this scripture in church and at home since I was a little girl. I always thought it was a nice scripture but I never realized its full impact until I met you. You have shown me love that can only be matched by God. When I got hurt, you could have turned away and no one would have blamed you or condemned you. But you chose to stay with me, and to love me against all odds." Jeremy shared her tears. "Your unselfish, sincere, love has helped me to recover. I appreciate you, and I will spend the rest of my life showing you just how much. I love you, Jeremy.

Lina lowered her camera and dried tears of her own. She looked around and found the majority of the wedding guests drying their eyes as well.

"This is the kind of love God has designed between a man and his wife, true unconditional love." Looking at Victoria and Jeremy, he continued. "God never promised us a perfect life, but He did promise us love. The love the two of you have for each other is representative of the love the Lord has for all of us."

Without hesitation, the officiant continued the ceremony. With professional precision, Lina snapped away. She was confident the couple would be pleased with the final results. Within minutes, the two became Mr. and Mrs. Jeremy Isaiah. A thunderous roar rang out as the guests clapped their hands in celebration. Maxwell joined in on the applause.

Chapter 22

Following the reception Maxwell loaded the equipment into his truck. The day had been long and exhausting. He could tell Lina was tired, but she didn't complain. "So working woman, are you hungry?" he asked.

"I am pretty hungry. I know you must be too." Lina turned to Maxwell and smiled. "Tell you what, since you have been such a wonderful assistant, how about I treat you to dinner."

Maxwell smiled. "That's kind of you to offer, but I can't let you pay for dinner. I'll take care of it. Where do you want to go?"

"I'm sort of in the mood for Mexican food. Can we go to Pepe's? Unless of course you prefer something different."

"Pepe's sounds good. As a matter of fact, I believe there is one pretty close to here." Maxwell pulled out from the parking lot and drove in the direction of the restaurant. His pocket buzzed indicating he had a telephone call.

"Are you going to get that? I know that buzzing has to be driving you crazy," Lina inquired. "You won't bother me by answering your phone."

"I'm sure whoever it is will leave a message. Simon is taking care of the store. I spoke to my mother earlier and she was straight, so I'm really not worried about it." Maxwell pulled into Pepe's parking lot. The lot was full. "It looks pretty packed in there."

"Yeah it does," Lina agreed. "Let's just get it to go. We can always eat our meal at my apartment. Besides it'll give us some time to talk."

Maxwell looked at her in disbelief. "Are you sure about that?"

"Yes I'm sure." Lina pursed her lips. I'm not going to do anything to you. I'm not that kind of woman."

Laughing, Maxwell agreed. "Okay, we can take it back to your place to eat, but don't make this a habit young lady."

"Forget you, let's get our food."

Maxwell and Lina rode to her apartment in silence. He couldn't believe Lina invited him to eat with her in such a private setting. He felt good seeing the direction their relationship was heading in. Although he was interested in becoming involved with her, he realized building trust was most important.

Arriving at her apartment, Lina muttered, "Home sweet home." She grabbed the food, and headed inside, as Maxwell gathered the equipment.

Lina set the table while Maxwell brought her equipment inside. It had been a long time since a man had been in her apartment. Normally she wouldn't invite a guy in but this was different. Maxwell had helped her out a lot. Plus, after the noise of the wedding reception, she wanted to sit in a quiet atmosphere to enjoy her meal.

Maxwell placed his jacket on the back of his chair. "Where can I go to wash my hands?" he asked.

"Oh, the bathroom is right through there." Lina pointed to a short hall on the other side of the apartment. "Just go straight back; the light should be on."

Lina grabbed two glasses from the cabinet and filled them with ice. "What would you like to drink?" she yelled to Maxwell. "I have iced tea, Coke, and water."

Maxwell returned to the kitchen, drying his hands on a

paper towel. "Coke will be fine." He sat down and watched as Lina filled his glass with the sparkling liquid. After Lina sat down opposite of him he looked at her with a hard stare.

"What?" she asked, before placing a forkful of enchiladas in her mouth.

"You know you were wrong today."

"Huh? What are you talking about?" She had an idea about what he was referring to but she wanted to hear him say it. She wanted to know exactly what he was thinking.

"You could have told me," he paused trying to find the right words to say. "About the bride's condition. I was not expecting that at all."

Shrugging her shoulders she replied. "There's a reason I didn't tell you."

Maxwell took a bite of his taco. Picking up a napkin, he wiped his mouth. "And what reason was that? I was completely caught off guard. I'm sure it reflected on my face. It was already weird being at a wedding for people I didn't know, but when you add that into the equation it was overwhelming, to say the least."

Nodding her head in agreement Lina said, "I can understand that. It would have been easy for me to share her condition with you on the way to the wedding. However, if I had done that you would have been waiting to see her condition instead of acknowledging the beauty of the moment." She picked up her glass and took a sip of iced tea. "It's just like the first time I saw the movie Titanic. I spent the first half of the movie waiting for the ship to sink because I knew it was coming. I later realized I had missed out on a beautiful love story, because I was waiting for the tragedy."

"That's pretty deep. When you put it that way, I can see your point." Maxwell nodded his head in agreement. "It was a nice ceremony. There were a lot of things I was able to take away from the experience. I was thinking, man this is a sermon all by itself."

"One thing that I have learned, Maxwell, is some of the most profound sermons we experience are shown and not spoken. Some of the greatest lessons are taught without words."

Maxwell acknowledged her statement. "I must say, Jeremy is a good man. Most men would have turned their back on her, but he stuck and stayed. You know God is going to bless him for that."

"I honestly believe He already has. The car accident didn't change who Victoria was as a person. It just changed her outer appearance." Lina spoke more to herself than she did to Maxwell. "The reality of life is beauty fades, but it's the qualities a person possesses on the inside that define the person."

Placing the last bite of food in his mouth, Maxwell squeezed his napkin tightly. "You know, we really take a lot for granted. It's amazing to see life through the eyes of others. You never know what people are dealing with until they allow you to see it firsthand."

Following dinner, Lina pulled up the original email message she received from Victoria and showed Maxwell her 'before' picture. With her eyes becoming glassy, she whispered, "This goes to show that your life can be completely changed in an instant." She knew that statement was true more than anyone.

The atmosphere in Lina's apartment became intense. Maxwell could tell Lina was deeply saddened but he didn't know why. He wanted to reach out to comfort her, but he thought better of the idea. Placing his hand on her shoulder he said, "It's getting pretty late, you've had a long day. Why don't you get some rest. I'm sure your body could use it." Hoping to lighten her mood, he said, "You worked pretty hard, and I know your feet are probably dying to get out of those shoes."

Lina laughed, "My tootsies really are crying. I guess we better call it a night."

Maxwell grabbed his suit jacket and walked towards the door. Lina joined him. "Thank you for everything, Lina. This has been an extraordinary day. I appreciate you sharing it with me."

"I wouldn't have had it any other way."

Maxwell smiled and extended an arm to give Lina a friendly hug. Much to his surprise, she accepted his motion and completed the hug. "Get some rest, okay. I hope to see you in the morning for church. Suddenly Maxwell's cell phone buzzed in his pocket, interrupting her response.

"You better get that. Goodnight, Maxwell." Lina closed the door, cleared the dishes from the table and retired to the bedroom. "Finally, I can get out of these dreadful shoes."

Chapter 23

Maxwell climbed into his vehicle and pulled out his cell phone. The low battery indicator was displayed across the screen. After plugging his phone into the car charger, he drove home.

He had so much on his mind. He turned the radio off so that he could focus only on his thoughts. Things between him and Lina were going even better than he expected. He liked the fact that things were moving slowly. He had been in enough bad relationships that he knew how to appreciate a good one. Lina was unlike any other woman he had met. She caught him completely off guard when she offered to buy dinner. Yep, Lina Fairweather was definitely a different type of woman.

****

I don't know what this man's problem is. I will not be ignored. Maxine had made several attempts to contact Maxwell since receiving his message, but to no avail. Not to be defeated, Maxine made a final attempt to contact him. She pulled out her phone and dialed his number. Sitting on her bed, she waited for his familiar voicemail greeting to play.

"Hello," Maxwell answered in a smooth baritone.

"Oh, Maxwell. You are there. I was just about to hang up."

"Hey, Maxine. How are you doing?"

"I'm much better now. Your prayers worked. My mother is doing so good, it's like she was never sick." *Actually she never was but you don't have to know that,* she thought.

"That's great. God is awesome." Maxwell pulled the phone

away from his ear so that Maxine couldn't hear him yawn. He didn't want to answer her call but he knew she would continue to call until she reached him. "How are things with you otherwise?"

"Otherwise things are good. My law firm has been taking on a lot of new clients, and I couldn't be doing better. It seems I'm always meeting with a client or going to court these days."

"I heard that. I'm happy for you."

"That's enough about me. What about you? What's going on in your world? I know one thing is for sure, you're a hard man to get in touch with." Maxine hoped Maxwell would give her some indication of what he had been up to.

"I'm sorry. I know you've had a hard time reaching me. What can I say? I'm a busy man. Between the church and the store I don't have a lot of time for much else."

"Is that all? I thought for sure you were going to tell me you had a girlfriend."

Here we go, Maxwell thought. He knew Maxine wasn't doing that much calling for nothing. "No, I don't have a girlfriend."

Maxine could sense a hint of irritation in his voice. Everything he was saying sounded good, but she was no dummy. Someone held Maxwell's attention and she was aiming to change that.

"Listen, Maxine. I'm sorry I'm not trying to be rude, but I'm very tired. I need to get some rest. I have service in the morning and Pastor James is depending on me to be on my A game."

"I understand; no need to apologize. I should be getting some sleep myself. I'll talk to you later."

"Thank you for understanding. You have a good night."

"I will. You do the same." Maxine ended her call with Maxwell and immediately sent a text message to Jason. "You haven't heard the last of me, Maxwell," she yelled as if he could hear her.

"Hey, Jason. This is Maxine. What did you say the name of the church Maxwell attends is?

Within minutes Jason replied to her message. "Christ the True Vine on 68th."

"Thanks, you're the best. xoxo"

"No problem."

Maxine typed the church name into her computer's search engine. Within seconds, the results provided her with a link to the church's website. She jotted down the street address and service times. Climbing under the covers, she displayed a wicked grin. "See you in the morning, Max."

****

Maxwell woke up with a smile on his face. He couldn't remember the last time he had slept so well. He couldn't wait to get to church to give God some praise.

At church, Maxwell danced around the pulpit, enjoying the sound coming from the choir. All was well in his world, and he was grateful to God. Looking out over the congregation, he could tell Lina was enjoying the service as well. She stood clapping and swaying along with the choir. She always seems so focused at church.

The choir completed their song and took a seat. Sunlight from the front door filled the sanctuary. Maxwell could not believe his eyes. Maxine entered the church wearing a red Herve Leger dress with crystal accents on the collar and buttons. A matching hat three times the size of her head added drama to her outfit, along with four inch, red sequin stilettos. Sashaying her way down the main aisle, she took a seat close to the front, blocking the view of several parishioners behind her. Looking up at Maxwell, she gave a slight wave.

Feeling uneasy, Maxwell glanced at Lina to gauge her reaction. He noticed Cheri whispering something in Lina's ear. *I don't believe this*, he thought. *This woman just won't quit.*

Pastor James rose to the podium and delivered a compelling message on unconditional love. "In Saint John chapter fifteen verse twelve, Jesus commands us to love one another as he has loved us. You see, children of God, you can't just love when it's convenient for you. You can't turn on love one minute and then when someone upsets you or something doesn't go your way you turn that love back off. That's not love."

Amen's could be heard all over the church.

"It amazes me how so many people say they love you but then when you need them, they're nowhere to be found. I once heard of a prominent television evangelist that took a stand saying it was okay for someone to divorce their spouse if that spouse was overtaken with Alzheimer's. What kind of foolishness is that? Love is an action, not just a feeling or emotion." Grabbing the microphone from the stand, Pastor James paced the length of the pulpit. "You say you have love. Can you love someone when they're down and out? Can you love someone when they disagree with a decision you've made. Can you love when things don't go your way? Can you continue to love when the answer is beyond your reach?"

Looking out over the congregation, Pastor James softened. "Children of God, true love, unconditional love only comes from God. We are living in such a cruel society. It seems as if trouble is around every corner. It is only with the love of Christ that we can make it. If we, as the children of God, don't show that love, who will. I implore you today to love. Show love when it's easy. Show even more love when it's hard. Remember the very one that you are withholding your love from is probably the one that needs it the most. Jesus said in Saint John fifteen and thirteen, 'Greater love has no man than this, that a man lay down his life for his friends.'

Pastor James returned to the podium. "Everyone stand to your feet." The congregation readily complied. "The message today was all about love. Love is something that each and every one of us can use more of. Some of you here today are the ones walking around withholding love for various reasons. Some of you have been hurt, embarrassed, and belittled. There are even some of you in here that may feel like nobody loves you. You've faced some horrible things in your life, and you feel love is not available to you. I'm here to tell you today, God is love. When you can't see love anywhere else, see the love of Christ. Let us leave here today not only receiving the love of Christ, but let's show that love. You never know whose life you could save just by showing love." Pastor James concluded his message with a prayer.

Following the Pastor's sermon, Maxwell was asked to offer the benediction. At the conclusion of the service, Maxine rose from her seat and hurriedly made her way to the front of the church. Maxwell noticed Cheri whispering in Lina's ear again. He could only imagine what she must have been saying.

Extending his hand, Maxwell offered Maxine a handshake. "Hi, Maxine," he said dryly."

"Boy, you better quit playing and give me a hug." She pushed his hand out of the way and enveloped her arms around him in a hug. Before loosening her embrace, she placed a kiss on the side of his face near his chin. Bright red lipstick lingered on his face like a tattoo. "I'll bet you're surprised to see me here. One of my girlfriends was telling me about this church, so I decided to visit today. Imagine my surprise when I walked in and saw you sitting in the pulpit."

"I'll bet you were surprised," he replied sarcastically. Maxwell searched for Lina in the crowd. He didn't want her to get the wrong idea about him and Maxine. He made eye contact with her just before she walked out the door.

Pastor James walked up, drawing his attention. "Minister Lee, who is this you have here?"

Maxwell turned in surprise. Apparently Maxine had caught the attention of a lot more than just Lina. "This is Maxine Miller, an old childhood friend of mine."

Pastor James offered Maxwell a handkerchief. "Uh Minister, you have a little something on your face."

Maxine smirked.

Maxwell took the handkerchief and wiped his face. Seeing the red lipstick on the handkerchief, he gave Maxine a sharp look. No wonder Lina and Cheri were whispering so much. Looking around the room, he noticed they had gained the attention of several parishioners.

"Oops, Maxwell. I'm sorry," Maxine lied. She knew exactly what she was doing. She was no fool she saw him constantly looking for someone. She wasn't going away that easily. Maxwell might as well get used to it. He better be glad she didn't join the church.

Pastor James could tell Maxwell was obviously uncomfortable. "Minister Lee, I hate to pull you away from your friend, but I need to see you in my office. I have some things I need to go over with you regarding the building project."

"Yes sir, Pastor. I'll be right there." Maxwell turned to Maxine. "I'm sorry, Maxine but will you please excuse me. I need to take care of some church business. I'll talk with you later."

"Aww, shoot. I was hoping we could grab a bite to eat," she replied, poking her bottom lip out.

Maxwell shook his head. "I'm sorry, but I already have plans. We'll have to get together some other time. Now if you'll excuse me. I have to go." He didn't wait for her response. Maxwell walked away quickly.

Maxine stood fuming.

Maxwell tapped on the door to the Pastor's study. "Pastor James you wanted to see me?" He asked, sticking his head inside the office.

Pastor James waved his hand, beckoning Maxwell forward. "Yes, son. Come on in here."

Maxwell stepped inside the pastor's office and took a seat across from Pastor James. Pastor James loosened and removed his neck tie. "Tell me, son, how are things going with you?"

"Things are good for me right now, Pastor. I honestly can't complain." Maxwell shifted in his seat. Whenever Pastor James called him son, he knew a deep conversation would follow.

"This is really none of my business, but you looked pretty uncomfortable out there today. One minute you were smiling, dancing, and praising God. Then the next minute you looked like you had seen a ghost. I don't know what's going on with you and that young lady but as the prospective pastor of Christ the True Vine there is a certain image you will need to uphold." Pastor James leaned back in his chair and folded his hands across his protruding belly.

"Pastor, it's not what you think at all. There is nothing, and I do mean nothing going on between me and her. She's just a girl I grew up with. I hadn't seen or heard from her since we were in junior high school. She saw my brother out and about one day, asked about me, and now I can't seem to get rid of her." Maxwell exhaled and shook his head in frustration.

"Well, son, when you step into the realm of ministry, the enemy will come against you with all that he has. Unfortunately, for men, a lot of times the enemy comes in the form of a woman. I can imagine for you it's even more difficult because you're single, and don't have the support of a companion." Pastor James chuckled. "I may be old, but I ain't blind, nor am I dumb. You're going to have to find a way to handle that sister. I can't put my finger on it, but something about her just doesn't sit right with me."

Maxwell didn't know what to make of his conversation with Pastor James. Maybe he saw something Maxwell hadn't seen. True enough, Maxine was pretty over the top, but she was still a good person. It didn't matter anyway. He had no interest in Maxine Miller. "Don't worry, Pastor. I'm good, trust me."

Pastor James sat up in his chair and placed his hands on the desk. "All right, son, I hear you. Just be careful. The members look at you as a leader. In all things, you must be an example."

Chapter 24

Maxwell pulled out his phone and dialed Lina's number. He regretted not being able to speak to her after church.

"Hello," she answered nonchalantly.

"Hey, Lina, this is Maxwell."

"I know who it is. What's up?"

Was that a hint of jealousy in Lina's voice, he wondered. An instant smile formed on his lips. "I'm sorry I didn't get to talk to you after service. I was glad to see you decided to come today."

"You were pretty busy after church. I don't even know how you managed to notice I was there."

"Are you okay, Lina? You seem a bit upset. Did I catch you at a bad time?" It took all the strength Maxwell had to keep from laughing. Lina always tried to appear uninterested when it came to him, but her tone was telling a very different story.

"I'm fine," she retorted. "What makes you think something is wrong?"

"Oh nothing, I'm just tripping I guess." Shifting gears, he asked, "So what are you up to?"

"Right now I'm working on the pictures from the wedding. I need to do some editing on them. Then I think I'm going to relax for the rest of the evening. Yesterday took a lot out of me." Lina's tone softened. "What about you?"

"I'm headed over to my mom's. After that I'm probably going to chill. This is one of those lazy days. You know what I'm saying."

"Yeah, I know what you mean." Lina paused for a moment. "I better get off this phone. I have a lot of work to do."

"Okay. Try not to work too hard." Maxwell ended his call with Lina feeling encouraged. He had hoped that whole scene with Maxine hadn't ruined his chances with Lina. What was that girl thinking anyway? He was sure she had given several people the impression that they were more than friends. "Lord, help me," he declared aloud.

Upon ending his call with Lina he called his mother. "Hey, Ma, what's up?"

Marilyn was glad to hear from her youngest son. "Not much, I'm just sitting around this house watching TV. What are you doing?"

"I'm actually on my way over there. Have you cooked, or do you want me to pick up something?"

"No, baby, I haven't cooked. I didn't know you were coming by. I can go in there and fix something right quick if you want me to."

"That's not necessary, I'll pick us up some Harold's."

"Harold's sounds good, baby. Get me a four piece wing dinner."

"Will do," he replied. Maxwell turned his vehicle in the direction of the restaurant. "I'll be there in little bit."

"Okay. I'll see you when you get here."

Maxwell pulled into the drive thru and ordered meals for both him and his mother. Marilyn's house was ten minutes from the restaurant. He hated to admit it but he needed his mother's guidance. He wanted to move things further along with Lina, yet he didn't want to move too fast. On the other hand, he had to do something about Maxine. He didn't want to be mean to her, but she was becoming unbearable.

Marilyn met Maxwell at the door. She greeted him with a hug and took the bags from his hand. "I'm going to get us some plates. Go on in there and wash your hands. I'll have this ready in a minute."

Shaking his head, Maxwell made his way to the bathroom. Thirty years old, and his mother was still telling him to wash his hands. Maxwell returned to find their meals sitting neatly on the table as if Marilyn had cooked them herself.

"This chicken is good, son. You got it exactly how I like it too. You know I love that Harold's mild sauce." Marilyn tore off a piece of chicken and popped it in her mouth. "So what's going on with you? I know you didn't come over here just to bring me chicken."

"Nothing too much," he said, peeling off a chunk of bread. "Let me get your opinion on something." Maxwell took a gulp of Pepsi. "Do you remember me telling you about a woman I met a few weeks ago?"

"Are you talking about the one you were supposed to be taking on a date?"

"Yeah, that's the one," he confirmed. We have gone out a couple of times since then. As a matter of fact, I attended a wedding with her yesterday."

"A wedding?" Marilyn inquired. "That's a pretty big deal isn't it?"

"No, it wasn't like that. She's a photographer, and she asked me to tag along as her assistant."

"Assistant, huh? Okay."

"Slow down, Ma. Let me finish telling you the story before you start jumping to conclusions."

Marilyn tried to read Maxwell's expressions. She wasn't sure who he was trying to convince more - her or himself. "I'm sorry, son. Go ahead."

"To be honest with you, Ma. I really do like this girl. She's nothing like the women I've dated in the past. In fact, I've been drawn to her since the first time I laid eyes on her. Now that I've had a chance to get to know her, I feel like she's the one."

"That's a big statement coming from you, son. What makes you think she's the one?"

"There's something about her. She doesn't try to put on a show for me. It's like she could care less about my possessions. She's just different." Maxwell dropped his head. "On the other hand, it seems like she's holding something back. I've noticed when she gets ready to open up and let me in, she puts this guard up. It's like she's afraid to allow herself to get too close to me."

"Maybe she's been hurt. She's probably just guarding her heart, trying to prevent a heartbreak."

"I wouldn't do that to her. I'm not that kind of guy," he stressed.

"I know that. Unfortunately for you, she doesn't know that. Pray about it. The Lord will show you what to do."

"Yeah, I guess you're right."

"What do you mean, you guess? Of course I'm right. I'm always right. I'm your mother," Marilyn joked.

Maxwell gave her a knowing glance. "Yeah, okay," he teased.

"Tell you what, bring her by here and let me meet her. I'll let you know whether or not she's worth all this stress you're putting yourself under."

"I'll see what I can do."

Maxwell finished his meal and went home. It was time he spent some alone time with God.

Chapter 25

Maxine fumed. She couldn't believe Maxwell blew her off like that. There wasn't one woman in that church that could hold a candle to her, but yet he treated her like she was nobody. And that pastor of his. Who did he think he was, interrupting them like that? How dare he give Maxwell that handkerchief. If it wasn't for him, Maxwell wouldn't have even known the lipstick was there. Those precious little church girls would have known he was mine then. That's okay. They got the point. God knows there were enough of them staring when she hugged him.

Judging by the look on his face when he saw her, Maxine assumed whoever the woman is that has his attention, was at church. Whoever she is, hopefully she got a good look at that hug and kiss.

Pulling the hat off her head, Maxine tossed it in the back seat. "I need a drink." Using the voice command feature on her car she called the one man she knew could never resist her.

"Hello."

"Hey, baby it's me. I need to see you. Meet me at my apartment in an hour," she demanded.

"I don't know if I can get away. She has been on my heels all day. What's going on?"

"Why does there have to be something going on for me to want to see you. Could it be that I want to spend some quality time with my man. You've been in meetings all week long so I couldn't come in your office like I normally do." Maxine pretended to pout.

"I know and I'm sorry. We've got people over here and everything. This is really not a good time. I can't get away."

"Oh you can, and you will get away. Don't act like you don't know what's waiting for you. I'll see you in an hour. I promise, it'll be worth your sacrifice. Trust me." Maxine ended the call and pressed harder on the accelerator. The roar of the engine sent her ego soaring. "That's what I thought," she whispered.

Maxine entered her apartment and changed out of her dress. Following a quick shower, she went into the kitchen and put a bottle of Dom Perignon in an ice bucket to chill. Removing two gold-rimmed Champagne flutes from the cabinet, she placed them on the ivory and gold coffee table. Finally, she took fresh strawberries and put them in a bowl next to the champagne. Satisfied with her efforts she stretched out on the couch and awaited Jonathan's arrival.

Her lips turned up into a seductive grin when the doorman buzzed her apartment. Using the remote control, Maxine turned on the radio and tuned in to the jazz station. She answered the door wearing a sheer black robe and black high-heeled slippers. "I see you figured out how to get away. I knew you would," she purred.

Jonathan stepped inside the apartment and admired Maxine's scantily covered body. "Turn around, baby and let me get a good look at you."

Maxine danced around slowly, basking in Jonathan's adoration. Reaching out she grabbed his hand and led him over to the couch. "Look what I prepared for you, baby."

Jonathan smiled broadly. "Look at you, taking care of your man."

Filling both glasses with champagne, Maxine relaxed in Jonathan's arms, inhaling his cologne. They sat quietly, enjoying the soulful sounds that reverberated throughout the room.

Unable to contain his desire for her any longer, Jonathan picked Maxine up and carried her off to the bedroom. Her laughter filled the apartment. "You are such a bad boy."

Chapter 26

"So, have you talked to Maxwell yet?" Cheri asked inquisitively.

"Yes, I talked to him."

"And."

"And what, Cheri."

"Don't play with me, Lina. Did he tell you who that chick was at church today or not?"

"We didn't talk about it. I didn't ask any questions and he didn't volunteer any information concerning her." Lina stated matter-of-factly. "It doesn't matter anyway. It's not like he's my boyfriend."

"Girl, please. If he's not your boyfriend the two of you sure have been acting like it. Every time I turn around, you're talking about Maxwell this, and Maxwell that. You may be able to put on a front for him, but I know you and I'm not buying it."

"Whatever, Cheri. You are always blowing stuff out of proportion. Maxwell and I are friends that's all nothing more, and nothing less."

Cheri became irritated. "I can't believe you're going to just sit up there and act like you don't have feelings for that man. Get real, Lina."

Lina was tired of going back and forth with Cheri. There was clearly no end in sight. "You know what," Lina surrendered. "I do like him, I'll admit that. I'm not trying to go there with him, though. I can't allow myself to get involved like that."

"Why not?" Cheri retorted. "You always say that, but you never say why. What's up with that, Lina. You're both single, and you're clearly attracted to each other. Plus whenever you talk about him, you light up like the Times Square Christmas tree."

"I just can't, Cheri. Now will you please drop it?"

"Okay, fine," Cheri surrendered.

"There is so much you don't understand Cheri," Lina pleaded.

"You said drop it, so I'm dropping it. Lord knows I have enough drama of my own. I don't have time to deal with yours too."

Silence filled the phone line. "Cheri," Lina spoke as if she had just remembered something. "How is it you were at church today? I thought you had to go out of town for your job. I wasn't expecting to see you until sometime next week."

"There was a last minute change of plans. The trip had to be postponed."

Lina became frustrated. "So, you're telling me you could have gone to the wedding with me after all."

"Oh, please. Girl, calm down. You were fine. You had all the help you needed with Maxwell being there," Cheri joked. "I'm sure he made a much better companion than I would have anyway."

"To tell you the truth, we did have a good time. I was glad he agreed to go with me. It was nice having a man to carry all that heavy equipment. And, girl let me tell you, he didn't let me lift a finger either. It felt too good," she bragged.

"Huh, I know it did. I ain't mad at you," Cheri replied.

Lina began telling Cheri about the wedding. In no time the friends were engulfed in conversation about something other than Maxwell Lee. Lina hated having to dodge Cheri's questions. She just didn't know how to explain things without disclosing too much about herself.

On top of it all, Cheri had roused her curiosity. Who was that woman at church? Lina had never seen her before and Maxwell had never spoken of her. She seemed awfully familiar with him though, practically kissing him on his neck in the church, of all places. And Maxwell, Lina didn't know why he constantly looked at her. He didn't have to answer to her. His reaction made him look guilty as sin.

****

The more Maxwell thought of Lina, the more frustrated he became. He wanted things to progress between them, but she hadn't given him any indication that she wanted the same thing. If he moved too fast, he could potentially run her off. On the other hand, if he didn't show her he wanted them to be more than friends soon, she might think he wasn't interested.

I've been out of the game way too long, he thought. It had been several years since his previous relationship. Maxwell met his ex-girlfriend in college. They had several mutual friends so it was no surprise when they met at a college party. After dating off and on for close to a year, they decided to make their relationship exclusive. They spoke of moving in together and eventually getting married. As they approached their senior year, Maxwell started to notice changes in her behavior. She became overly argumentative and started spending less time with him.

When he confronted her about the changes in their relationship, she immediately became defensive. She told him he was being paranoid and needed to chill out. Each day seemed to bring new problems and more arguments. Ultimately, the issues in their relationship caused a divide among their friends.

Maxwell felt as though he had to defend himself to his girlfriend and their female friends as well.

Eventually he decided enough was enough. He was tired of trying to mend a relationship that was clearly beyond repair. They tried to remain friends after the breakup but too much damage had been done. The last he'd heard was that she had taken a job in Los Angeles in broadcasting.

Once he ended his relationship, Maxwell decided he would date various women but not commit to a serious relationship. His commitment to church and his business made avoiding relationships easier. He convinced himself he was too busy to get seriously involved.

He held true to his declaration, until Lina Fairweather walked into his life. It was almost ridiculous how quickly he became attracted to her. Something about her drew him to her. He couldn't explain it. Whatever it was, he knew a woman like Lina didn't come along every day.

As fond of Lina as he was, his irritation with Maxine was equally as intense. Thoughts of her actions at church sent waves of anger throughout his mind. He couldn't believe the display she put on in front of the congregation. It was no surprise to him when Pastor James joined them. Had he been in Pastor James' position he would have done the same thing.

Maxwell's mind raced. He needed guidance. Closing his eyes, Maxwell sought the one he knew could help. He prayed within, *Lord, you said in your Word I could ask anything in your name and it shall be given to me. Heavenly father, I ask you to give me wisdom and guidance concerning my life. Help me to know those that you desire to be a part of my life, and also those that I should avoid. These things I ask in your son Jesus' name. Amen.*

After concluding his prayer, Maxwell relaxed in his recliner and turned the television on to the nine o'clock news broadcast. The telephone rang, drawing his attention. He looked at the display with a bit of confusion. It was unusual for Pastor James to call him late in the evening, especially on a church night. Without hesitation, he answered the call.

Pastor James' husky voice rattled on the other end. "I didn't wake you did I, son?" he asked.

"No, Pastor, you didn't wake me. I was just sitting here watching the news."

"Oh, I see. Is there anything interesting on?"

"Nothing but the same stuff that's always on," he replied. "I normally only watch it to hear the weather report for the week, to be honest with you."

Maxwell could hear Pastor James clearing his throat on the other end. After a short pause, he got to the main reason for his call. "Son, I know I already talked to you after service today. But I was sitting in my study reading the Word and you came across my mind. At first I tried to shake it off and move on, but I couldn't," he explained. "I've noticed you've been a bit distracted during services lately. Now don't get me wrong, I'm not accusing you of any wrong doing. That's not what I mean by distracted."

"I didn't think that, Pastor," Maxwell stated.

"You know I'm not the kind of man that will beat around the bush. That's not my nature, never has been. I'm just going to come right out and ask you. Does the reason you've been so distracted have anything to do with the young lady that has been attending the services with Sister Cheri? I've noticed you looking fondly in her direction quite a bit during service."

"You mean Lina?" he asked.

"Oh, is that her name? I'm not sure I ever knew her name."

"Yes, sir, that's her name."

"The fact that you know her name alone brings me to my next question. Are you and her involved?"

Maxwell frowned at the pastor's boldness, but at the same time, he wanted to see where he was going with his line of questions. No, Pastor, Lina and I aren't involved. We're just friends. What makes you ask about her?" Maxwell wondered why Pastor James seemed so adamant about learning about the meaning of his relationship with Lina.

"Well, son, I've noticed the way you look at her. I know you're a single man and I understand your desire for God to bless you with a wife." Pastor James was careful in the way he spoke to Maxwell. He didn't want to discourage him. "You know the way you look at her reminds me of the way I looked at my wife when we met all those years ago. There was something about her. Believe it or not, the situation was similar. Although I wasn't a minister, I was in the church, and I remember the day she walked through the door. I couldn't let her leave without talking to her. I was afraid I might not see her again. We've been together ever since."

"Whoa, slow down, Pastor," Maxwell interrupted. "It ain't like that. Really, we're just friends. We haven't even committed to dating. We're not on that level."

"Son, I was once young, and now I've gotten to be an old man. But I'm not too old to see what's going on," Pastor James stressed, "I'm certainly not too old to know when a man cares for a woman. I don't know who you're trying to convince, me or yourself, but I know what I know." Pastor James paused as if he was trying to find the right words to say. "Let me tell you something. Sometimes in life things don't play out the way we desire for them to. Some things simply take time. I just want to encourage you today to remember that whatever your heart's desire is, God will give it to you."

Turning serious, Pastor James continued, "I wouldn't be right if I didn't tell you that not every blessing is wrapped in a perfect package. Not every blessing comes easy. Some things we have to work for. Now you be encouraged. God is going to bless you, in His time."

Maxwell considered Pastor James' words. He respected him not only as his pastor but he also looked up to him as his elder. "Thank you, Pastor. I receive that. I believe God is going to bless me. As a matter of fact I'd even venture to say, any way He sees fit to bless me, I'll be satisfied."

"Be careful, son. Those words carry a mighty weight."

"I'm just saying, I know God has good things in store for me and I'm willing to wait for Him to bring it to pass. I appreciate you taking the time to call me and share this with me, Pastor. It means a lot to me."

"Son, I'm praying for you. My wife is praying for you also. You're a young man, and you're a single man. Like I told you once before, we're looking forward to the day when you can take over as pastor and carry this ministry to the level that God intends for it to go. But now I'm going to tell you, especially after what I saw today, you definitely are going to need a help mate." Pastor James laughed.

Maxwell joined him in laughter. "I hear you, Pastor. I hear you."

Pastor James inhaled deeply, and slowly expelled the air through his lips. "Alright, young man. I guess I've done enough talking for the night. It won't be long before the missus comes looking for me. It's about time for us to watch our regular show on television and lay it down for the night. It was good to talk to you, and I'll be talking with you soon. You have a good night.

"Okay, Pastor. It was good to talk to you too. Tell Mother James I said hello." Maxwell ended the call.

Looking up towards the ceiling, Maxwell shook his head. "Hmm, God," he said. "What are you trying to tell me? Moments ago I was praying, asking you for direction. Before I could get through praying good, Pastor James calls me out of the blue asking about Lina. Lord, I don't want to read too much into anything. To be honest with you, Lord. I'm more confused than I was when I started." He laughed within himself. "Some stuff only happens to me," he declared before turning in for the night.

Chapter 27

"Where on earth could my lens be?" Lina searched frantically through her equipment looking for her wide-angle lens. "I know I had it, where could it be?" she shrieked.

She had one hour before she was scheduled to meet with her newest client, the director of Southside Children's Museum. The museum's director contacted Lina at the request of one of her colleagues. Lina had seen a substantial increase in her clientele within the past few months. She gave complete credit to God. She was asked to shoot photos to be used in new promotional materials for the museum. It was unusual for her to misplace her equipment; she was normally organized.

As if she had the wind knocked out of her, it occurred to her. "Oh no...Maxwell," she murmured. "It has to be in his truck. I have looked everywhere. In fact, I have turned this place upside down. That's the only thing that makes sense. He must still have it." Lina pulled her cell phone from her pocket and dialed Maxwell's number.

"Hello," Maxwell's heavy voice came across the line.

"Maxwell, this is Lina. Did I disturb you?" she asked.

"Not at all. What's going on?" Maxwell tried to play it cool, but within he was excited. It was rare for her to call him. He was normally the one doing the calling.

"I'm sorry, Maxwell."

"You don't have to apologize for calling. I look forward to hearing from you."

"I've looked everywhere, and...but I can't find my wide-angle lens anywhere. The only thing I can think of is maybe I left it in your truck. Maybe it rolled under the seat when you put the boxes in there the other day. Could you please check for me?" she pleaded.

"Uh, I don't recall seeing it, but I'll go and check."

"Oh, Maxwell, that would be great. I have a photo shoot in an hour. If it's not in your truck, I don't know what I'll do."

"Calm down, Lina. Everything will be okay. Give me a second to put some shoes on and I'll run out and look." Maxwell was preparing for work when Lina called. He was scheduled to open up the store this morning but there was no way he was going to leave her in distress. Slipping his feet into a pair of loafers, he went out to the garage and searched inside the truck. "I'm so sorry," he said.

"What," Lina asked, exasperated. "Please don't tell me you didn't find it."

"I was going to say I'm so sorry, it must have slipped out of the box. It's right here."

"Oh my God, Maxwell, I could kiss you right now."

"That sounds good," he teased.

"Don't even try it. You can't take that literally." Lina giggled in the phone, "Look at you trying to take advantage of a situation."

"I'm just messing with you. Relax." Maxwell paused for a thought. "Tell you what, I'll throw on something real quick and bring it to you. After all, it's my fault. That's the least I could do."

"Would you really do that for me?" she asked surprised by his offer.

"I don't want you to come all the way over here and then rush to your photo shoot Give me about twenty minutes, and

I'll be there.

"Thank you, Maxwell," She declared repeatedly. "When you get here I'll be ready to leave."

"Sounds like a plan. I'll see you in a little while."

Lina gathered the remainder of her equipment and loaded up the car. She waited patiently for Maxwell's arrival.

Maxwell put on a pair of jeans and a t-shirt and prepared to leave. He knew time was an issue, therefore, he wasn't able to dress for work the way he normally would. He grabbed a suit out the closet and a pair of shoes. Hanging the suit in the back of his truck, he headed out. *I'll get dressed at the store*, he thought. As promised, within twenty minutes he pulled up to Lina's apartment.

Lina watched frantically from the window, anticipating his arrival. When she saw his Escalade pulling up, she dashed out the door, and quickly locked it behind her.

"Slow down, girl," Maxwell teased. You could fall and break your neck."

"You have no idea how much this means to me." Lina reached out and gave him a light squeeze. "Thank you so much," she exclaimed. To his surprise, she kissed him on the cheek. "Now, Mr. Lee, there's your kiss," she joked.

"And what a great kiss it was," he retorted.

"Maxwell."

"What can I say, I'm a man," he replied, smiling. He extended his hand, and offered her the lens. "Here's your lens, now go. You don't want to be late."

Lina snatched the lens from his hand. "Thanks. You have no idea how much this means to me. I owe you one." Jumping in her car, she pulled off quickly.

Maxwell stood and watched as her car disappeared. "Wow."

He shook his head then looked at his watch. He needed to get going as well.

Lina looked in her rearview mirror sneaking one last glance at Maxwell. "Uh, uh, umm," she whispered. "That is one fine man." Even in jeans and a t-shirt, he was handsome. She didn't know what came over her. Hugging him and kissing him on his cheek was unexpected and totally out of her character. As much as she tried to fight it, she knew her feelings for Maxwell were becoming stronger and they were getting harder to fight. *Oh God, how do I get myself into these situations?* "I have to stop this. I have to find a way to get away from Maxwell Lee before one of us gets hurt," she declared aloud. Her mind told her she needed to end things, but her heart said otherwise. There was no way she was ready to let go.

Chapter 28

Maxwell arrived at the store thirty minutes before the mall opened. He stepped into his office and changed clothes. *Man, the things you do for a woman.* Smiling he thought, *But it's worth it.* He didn't know where his relationship with Lina would end up. He tried not to ponder the thought. He enjoyed where they were.

Busying himself around the store, he struggled to keep thoughts of Lina at bay. He couldn't allow her to consume his mind to the point that it would interfere with his work performance. Going over reports and figures, he was pleased with the store's progress. His staff had stepped up their sales efforts and his customer base was increasing. Many of the businessmen and preachers from Chicago's South Side, and surrounding areas, frequented the store. He accredited his success to quality merchandise and excellent customer service.

"Hey, Max, what's going on?" Jason tapped on the door before entering Maxwell's office.

"Hey, man, come on in. What're you up to?" Maxwell waved at Jason, beckoning him into the office.

Jason plopped down on the chair in front of Maxwell's desk. "Man, nothing. I'm taking a quick break. How's everything going?" Jason asked.

Maxwell leaned forward on the desk, "Aw, man let me tell you. I hate you ever gave ole girl my phone number. As a matter of fact, I hate you ever even ran into that girl."

Surprised, Jason said, "Who are you talking about?"

Giving Jason a blank stare, Maxwell continued. "Man, I'm talking about Maxine. That woman is something else," he stressed.

Jason looked stunned. "What did she do?" he asked, sounding confused.

"Man, it's more like what didn't she do. Number one, every time I turn around she's calling. I mean, you'd think she would take the hint by me barely returning her calls. Not her, she's constantly calling." Leaning back, Maxwell smiled. "Now that wouldn't be a bad thing if I was looking at her like that, but I'm not. Last week she called me and said her mother was sick and she needed prayer. I'm beginning to wonder if that was even true."

"For real, dawg?"

Maxwell gave him a knowing look. "Dude, she showed up at my church."

"Your church?" Jason repeated in disbelief. "That must be why she texted me Saturday night."

In his animation, Maxwell disregarded Jason's response.

"She was all out there. Don't get me wrong, she was dressed to the nines. She drew plenty attention, just not good attention. Man, that girl even drew the Pastor's attention. Then on top of that, she had the nerve to kiss me and leave lipstick all over me. Right there in the middle of the church. Pastor James had to point it out to me. I didn't even know it was there. Who does that?"

Jason laughed. "Aw, man, I didn't know you were about to end up with a stalker. I mean she was cool back in the day." Jason looked at Maxwell like he was trying to piece together a puzzle. "What's going on with you, Max?" he asked. "I mean, you've seen the girl." Reminiscing, Jason smiled. "I've seen her. Why are you avoiding her anyway? Especially if she's feeling you like that."

Maxwell dropped his voice slightly above a whisper. "I have other things on my mind right now."

"Other things, or another woman? What's up?"

Laughing slyly, Maxwell said, "There is this one lady that I've been spending a little time with. We're at that friend stage for now. Man, I have to admit, I'm feeling her. In fact, I'm developing some pretty strong feelings for her."

"What? It's like that?" Jason said, stressing his words.

"Yeah, bruh; it's like that."

"All snap. She has to be fine, if you're passing up an opportunity to be with Maxine."

"She is. She's a beautiful woman, but her beauty is not what attracts me the most. She has a personality out of this world. She is so real with everything that she does. She doesn't try to be more than who she is. She's not the type to try to boost herself up. She has one of those take me as I am type attitudes."

"Man, that's good. I hope everything works out for you." Jason was surprised. He hadn't seen Maxwell get this excited about a woman since he was in college. Whoever this woman was, she had to be pretty special to his little brother. "What are you going to do about this Maxine situation?" he asked.

Taking a deep breath, Maxwell forced the air out, hoping to relieve the stress. "I don't know. The only thing I know to do is to let it ride. Being in the position I'm in, I can't hurt her feelings. I have to handle this situation real delicately. What if she is genuinely trying to get closer to the Lord? Which I doubt, but who am I to judge. I can't be the one to turn her away from that." Frustrated, Maxwell continued. "I don't know how I'm going to handle it. One thing's for sure, I *will* handle it."

"I hear you," Jason replied.

Changing the subject, Maxwell asked, "When's the last time you stopped by mom's house? You know she be wanting to see you."

"Rolling his eyes, Jason replied, "Here you go. I was wondering when you would get to it. Dude, I'm not trying to go over there." Evidence of Jason's frustration displayed on his face. Wrinkling his forehead, he continued. "Every time I go over there, Mama starts tripping. She always finds a way to pick at me and I know it's because of my father. All that mess that went down between them was a long time ago. Yet, she still tries to hold it against me. I realize he put her in danger multiple times because of his criminal activity, but that was a long time ago. I wish she would just let it go. I'm a grown man now, and I'm tired of hearing it. I'm not going to deal with it. So to keep from hurting her feelings or being disrespectful I simply keep my distance."

"Jason, we only have one mother." Maxwell pleaded. "We don't know how much longer we'll have her either. She could live another forty years. Then again, she could be gone tomorrow. The Bible tells us to honor our fathers and our mothers, man." Softening, Maxwell continued. "I realize everything is not always cool between you and her. You may not have the best relationship, but man, you can change that. Don't get me wrong, I know it's not only up to you, and it's not only up to her. It's up to both of you. Somebody is going to have to take a stand. One of you is going to have to step up. She's your mother man, she loves you."

"Yeah, miss me with that," Jason replied angrily. "I'll believe she loves me when I see it."

"Man, don't act like that."

"I'm serious, Max." Jason barked. "If I wanted a sermon I would have went to the church. I didn't come in here for this."

"Okay, all right." Maxwell decided to drop the subject. If nothing else, he knew he had given Jason something to think about. Changing subjects again, he asked. "How is work going?"

"It's all good."

"What about that special project you've got going on?"

Jason softened and displayed excitement. Rubbing his hands together, he said. "Everything's going to come out in the open. It's only a matter of days. I'll keep you up on it."

Maxwell nodded his head and smiled. "Okay, I'll wait for the announcement then."

"Yeah, little bruh, wait on it." Jason gave Maxwell the parting shot before returning to work.

Chapter 29

"Please pick up," Cheri begged. To her dismay, there was still no answer. "This makes no sense," she declared. "I know she's there." Cheri pressed the button to end the call on her phone. She had already left numerous voicemail messages, all of which had gone unanswered. *Why would she pull this when I'm not there to check on her?* With her frustrations mounting, Cheri decided to try the number once again. She became more upset with each passing ring. After four unanswered rings the familiar voicemail greeting played. She had heard it so much she could recite it on her own.

"Lina, where are you? I have been calling you for three days. What on earth are you doing, girl? I'm starting to get worried. Call and let me know you're all right." Cheri ended the call and tossed her cell phone on the king sized hotel bed. She was out of town at a weeklong convention for her job. She and Lina spoke briefly before she left Chicago but they hadn't spoken since. Lina told her that her schedule had picked up significantly but this was ridiculous.

She was out of ideas. Unable to make sense of their lack of communication, Cheri made one more desperate phone call. This time she was successful. Almost immediately, Maxwell answered.

"Hello," Maxwell answered cautiously.

"Maxwell, I mean, Minister Lee. This is Cheri. I got your phone number out of the church directory."

Hearing the desperation in her voice, Maxwell felt unnerved.

"What's going on, Cheri. You sound upset."

"I'm sorry to call you in such a panic, but I didn't know who else to call. Have you talked to Lina lately?" she asked.

"No, not since last week. Why?" He asked. "Is everything all right?"

"Yes. No. I don't know." Cheri stumbled over her words. She didn't want to alarm Maxwell unnecessarily, but her nerves were getting the best of her. "I'm out of town, and I've been trying to reach her for three days. She hasn't responded to any of my calls, voicemails, or text messages. I'm going crazy with worry. I was hoping you had at least talked to her. I don't want to call her parents because I don't want them to get worried over what could be nothing."

Maxwell listened attentively. When he hadn't heard from Lina, he figured she was either extremely busy or she needed some space. He didn't want to overwhelm her, the way Maxine had been overwhelming him.

"Cheri, I want you to calm down. You're going to make yourself sick over what could be nothing. I'll tell you what, I'm off work today. I'll go check on her. There could be a number of reasons why she hasn't returned your calls. Once I get there, and check things out, I'll give you a call back. Can I reach you at this number that's showing up on my phone?"

"Yes, this is my cell phone. I'll keep it on, so I'll know when you call. Please, Minister Lee, call me as soon as you get to her apartment."

"I will."

Without hesitation, Maxwell grabbed his keys and phone and left for Lina's apartment. He tried to keep his emotions intact. He didn't want to walk into a situation that would leave him upset or embarrassed. Every traffic light seemed to turn red as he approached it. With frustrations mounting, he banged his hands on the steering wheel. *I am way too caught up,* he thought. Unsure of what he was about to face, he whispered a short prayer. He prayed for Lina's safety and for his and Cheri's peace of mind.

Upon arriving at Lina's apartment, he circled the resident only parking lot to see if her vehicle was there. An ounce of relief swept through him when he saw the blue Chevy Cobalt parked in its normal spot. Pulling out of the parking lot, he drove around the corner and parked in front of her apartment. Maxwell approached the door cautiously, not knowing what to expect. He rang the doorbell and waited for a response. After standing outside for several minutes he alternated between ringing the doorbell and banging on the door.

"Hold on," he heard faintly. "I'm coming."

Maxwell noticed the curtain shift, indicating someone had peeked outside. Seconds later, he heard the turn of locks.

"Hi, Maxwell," Lina said weakly.

Taken aback, Maxwell stared at Lina, surprised. "Are you okay?" he asked.

"I'm fine, I just have a bad cold. Come on in." Lina coughed and stepped aside for Maxwell to enter.

Maxwell looked around the apartment and noticed a box of Kleenex, a bottle of hand sanitizer, and a can of Lysol sitting on the table in front of the couch. A small garbage can sat on the floor next to the table. Several blankets were pushed into the corner on one end of the couch.

Lina locked the door and returned to the couch.

"How long have you been sick?" he asked.

"A few days," she replied. Grabbing several Kleenex from the box, she sneezed multiple times and tossed the used tissues. Immediately she filled her hands with sanitizer and sprayed

Lysol.

"I came by here because Cheri called me. She said she had been trying to reach you for three days and that you hadn't responded."

I misplaced my phone the other day when I went to the grocery store. I wasn't feeling well so I came straight home instead of going to the cell phone place. It may even be somewhere here in the apartment. I haven't felt like looking for it. I was planning to go and get it replaced when I felt better."

"That explains why neither of us has heard from you," he stated. Lina appeared fragile to him. "I promised Cheri I would call her as soon as I got over here, so I better do that. That poor girl has been freaking out."

"I'm sorry," Lina whispered.

Maxwell removed his phone from his pocket and dialed Cheri. She answered immediately. He detailed for her Lina's condition and promised to keep her updated.

"Have you eaten anything, Lina?" He asked concerned.

"Not really. I don't have much of an appetite. Plus, I'm too tired to fix anything."

"No wonder you're so weak," he attested. "You never will fight off that cold if you don't eat and keep your fluid intake up. Have you been drinking fluids on a regular basis?"

"Yes, Dr. Lee, I have." Even though she was ill, Lina continued to show her witty side.

"Let me get you something to eat."

"You don't have to do that," she protested.

"I insist. Now lie down and let me take care of you."

"Those are mighty big words, Mr. Lee."

Maxwell walked over to the kitchen and searched the cabinets. Spotting a can of chicken noodle soup and a box of crackers, he removed them from the cabinet and looked for a pot. With little effort, he found everything he needed to both prepare and serve Lina a much needed meal.

"Thank you," she said sitting up and retrieving the plate containing a bowl of soup and crackers from Maxwell's hand.

"No problem, sweetheart. Is there anything else I can do for you?"

Lina lifted a spoonful of hot soup to her lips. Stopping short of her mouth, she looked at Maxwell confused. "What did you say?" she asked.

"I asked if there was anything else I can do for you," he replied nonchalantly.

"Oh, okay." She waited to see if he would call her sweetheart again, or if the cold had her hearing things. "No, I'm fine. You've already done enough, honestly."

Maxwell started to sit down in the chair across from Lina but stopped short. "I hate to ask you this, but would you mind if I used your restroom. I had a big cup of coffee on the way over here."

"Yeah, sure. You remember where it is. Make sure you aim straight and don't leave my seat up," she joked.

"Is there anything else I need to remember before proceeding to the restroom, miss?" he replied matching her wit.

"No, that will be all," she said, waving him off with her spoon.

Maxwell entered the restroom and made sure he followed all of Lina's instructions. Reaching for the hand soap, he accidentally knocked a medicine bottle off the counter. He washed his hands and reached for the bottle. He wanted to be sure to return it to its proper place. Seeing Lina's name on the prescription label drew his attention. The drug name Atripla was listed below her name and dosing instructions. *I wonder what this is for*, he thought. He knew he had heard the name before but couldn't recall where. *Probably some kind of allergy medicine*, he resolved.

Rejoining her in the living room, he noticed Lina had placed the plate containing her meal on the table. "Are you finished already?" he asked, pointing to the plate. "You must have been hungry."

"I guess I was," she agreed.

Maxwell retrieved the dishes and took them into the kitchen. After he had washed and put away everything, he walked back over to Lina. "Now that I know you have been sufficiently nourished, and properly hydrated, I'm going to get out of here. Since you've lost your phone, I'll drop back by tomorrow to check on you."

"Thank you, Maxwell," Lina said, pushing the blankets back so that she could get up to lock the door.

"Lina, what is that under your couch?" he asked.

Stepping over to the couch, he leaned down and picked up the small, black object. "Here's your phone," he said extending it to her. The screen was completely black.

"It must have fallen under there the other day when my purse fell off the table. Thank you, Maxwell."

"No problem. I'm sure you'll need to put it on the charger." Relieved, he said, "Since you have your phone now, I'll just call to check on you. If you need me, I'll come back over. Keep that phone near you, okay."

"I will. Thank you again for everything." Lina followed Maxwell to the door, locking it behind him.

Lina walked to her bedroom to retrieve her phone charger. The bathroom door was open. She decided to take a quick peek inside to see if Maxwell had let the seat down. "Oh, no," she cried, dropping her cell phone on the floor. On the counter in plain sight was her HIV medication. Immediately, tears streamed down her face, meeting under her chin. "He knows," she whispered.

Chapter 30

Lina collected herself and got up from the floor. She picked up her cell phone and proceeded to put it in the bedroom on the charger. Her mind raced as she thought about her secret being revealed to Maxwell. The fact that he didn't mention it unnerved her. On the other hand, the bottle did explain his sudden desire to leave. How would she ever be able to face him again? What would he think of her now that he knew?

Lina's mind filled with what ifs. What if she had mentioned her condition to him earlier? How would he have reacted? What if he never speaks to her again? What if he doesn't give her an opportunity to explain? Her mind raced in every direction. She knew Maxwell was a nice guy, but she also realized there was only so much a person could take. *Lord, please let me get a chance to explain*, she prayed. Lina sobbed, causing her to cough uncontrollably. "There's nothing I can do about it now," she declared. Climbing into her bed, she curled up into a ball and cried herself to sleep.

Maxwell left Lina's house feeling content. He was relieved knowing nothing horrible had happened to her. However, he did feel bad about her being so sick. He was glad he was able to go and check on her when Cheri called. He was even happier when she allowed him to take care of her. He couldn't believe he slipped and called her sweetheart. Even though he felt it in his heart and thought of it often, he wasn't ready to reveal something of that magnitude to Lina. He panicked when she drew attention to it. Not knowing what to say, he simply omitted that part when she asked him to repeat what he had said.

Taking care of her sent his mind into a tailspin. Is this what it would be like if they were married and she got sick? Would she give him the same care and concern if he was the one sick? Watching her fragile body consume the soup and juice that he prepared for her made him feel good. He couldn't imagine what would have happened to her if he hadn't gone by to check on her. There's no telling how long she would have gone without eating. He prayed silently for her. In addition to praying for Lina, he prayed for himself also. Praying he wouldn't be consumed by the germs that filled the room. *Hopefully that can of Lysol did what it needed to do*, he thought. *If not, I'm in trouble.* As a precaution, Maxwell stopped by the grocery store and purchased a gallon of orange juice, several fruits and vegetables and a few cans of soup. Grabbing a bottle of cold medicine, he completed his transaction and headed home. If he did happen to get sick, he would be prepared.

Maxwell arrived home and put away his groceries. Fatigued by the day's events, he decided to sit down and rest. Before he could sit, his phone rang, drawing his attention. Looking at the display, he recognized the familiar name and number.

"Hey, Ma," he answered.

"Maxwell, where are you?" she asked. Her frustration displayed in her tone.

"Huh?" he replied, confused by her obvious anger.

"I said, where are you? I've been sitting here waiting for you all day. Since I hadn't heard anything I figured I better call you. Did you forget you were supposed to be cleaning my gutters today? We planned it days ago."

"Ah, man, Ma, I forgot. I'm sorry. It completely slipped my mind. Give me a little while. I'll be over there soon."

"Okay," she conceded. "I'll see you when you get here."

Marilyn disconnected the call without saying goodbye.

"What is it with the women in my life today?" Maxwell declared.

A short time later, he arrived at his mother's house. She was in the living room watching her favorite game show. "It's about time you got here," she said, looking up at Maxwell as he walked through the door.

"Ma, I'm sorry. Please don't start."

"What?" she exclaimed.

"I didn't mean that the way it sounded. I've had a rough day."

"What do you mean, you had a rough day. Isn't this your day off?" she assessed.

"It is, but I got a phone call today from Lina's friend. She hadn't heard from Lina in a few days and she was all panicked. I hadn't heard from her either, so I said I would go by and check on her since we couldn't get her on the phone."

Marilyn's voice softened. "Is everything okay?"

"She's sick with a bad cold. Hopefully it's not the flu. We couldn't get her on the phone because she had misplaced her cell phone. Before I left I found it under the couch." Maxwell waved his hands in the air showing he didn't want to talk about it anymore. "Anyway, I'm here now."

Marilyn grabbed Maxwell's arm and pulled him down next to her on the couch. Looking him in the eye she asked, "You really care for this woman, don't you?"

"I don't know, Ma. I guess.

"No, there's no guessing to it, you really care for her. She means a lot to you. For you to go over on your day off and take care of a sick woman, she's more than a friend. You may tell me she's just a friend, and you may even try to convince yourself, but your heart is telling a different story."

"I felt so bad seeing her laying there sick. I almost felt helpless. I fixed her a little something to eat and gave her some juice, but I seriously hope she starts feeling better."

"She will. But that was kind of you to do what you did. I hope she appreciated it."

Maxwell stood. "Yeah, well, I'm gonna go and get started on these gutters."

"All right, you go on, and I'll go and get you a bottle of water."

Maxwell headed outside to work on the gutters. He felt torn. He knew he had made his mother a promise, but his mind and his heart was with Lina.

I should have stayed with her, he thought. Smiling at the thought of caring for her he whispered, "In sickness and in health."

Chapter 31

Maxwell entered the townhouse dragging. Every muscle in his body ached. He was physically exhausted. Climbing into the shower, he turned the water on as hot as he could stand it. The massaging showerhead added some relief to his tired muscles. Hard streams of water beat across his neck and back. "This has been a day," he moaned. Reflecting back on the day, he thought, *I was busier today than I am when I have to go to work. I'll have to remind myself not to take a day off.* Four hours of cleaning gutters is not the way he envisioned his day off. Taking care of Lina ended up being the easy part of the day. He had reached his physical limit. After completing his shower, he stepped into a pair of pajama pants and climbed into the bed. Sleep overtook him quickly.

Upon rising the next morning, Maxwell could feel the impact of the previous day. His muscles still ached and he was somewhat tired. "No rest for the weary," he declared as he sat up on the side of the bed. Picking up the remote control, he turned on his bedroom television and tuned it to the morning news. He frequently listened to the news as he prepared for work each day. He liked to listen for the weather report, and to hear the morning reports about what was going on in and around the city. There were always stories about crimes that were committed overnight. In addition, there was good news also. Some stories were funny, and some didn't make sense at all. With Chicago being a big city, there was always some type of festival or gathering going on. Maxwell enjoyed the easy banter among the news anchors. He stepped into his walk in closet to select a suit to wear for the day.

GlaxoSmithKline HIV drug beats Gilead's Atripla in study. After the break.

Maxwell tore out of the closet and stood in front of the television. "What, what did they just say?" he questioned aloud in utter disbelief. He waited impatiently for the commercials to end and for the newscast to begin again. After what seemed like an eternity to him, the broadcast resumed. The news anchors covered several stories that were insignificant to him. "Will you please get to the story," he yelled.

Now, in health news. GlaxoSmithKline's HIV drug, Dolutegravir proved to be more effective than Gilead Sciences' Atripla based on results obtained from testing done on 88% of study participants.

"Oh, my God," he whispered. Maxwell's mind began to spin. He tried to think back to when he was at Lina's house, and the medication he saw on the sink. *What was that?* he thought. He hoped to see how Atripla was spelled so that he could eliminate the possibility of it being the medication that Lina was prescribed. Unable to make sense out of the newscast, he pulled up the internet browser on his phone. Going into the search engine, he typed the letters a-t-r-i-p-l-a into the search line and pressed Enter. Immediately, results popped up. He held his breath as he read the top line. *Atripla - A one pill, once a day HIV treatment option.* Maxwell dropped his phone as if it was poisonous.

"There's no way. There is absolutely no way Lina could be infected. She would have told me." Growing angry, he continued, "Or would she? I can't believe this. I can't believe she would do this to me. How could she?" Fury boiled within Maxwell. "I don't believe I fell for somebody like that. Why

God," he yelled. Don't I deserve to have a good woman? Haven't I served you the way I'm supposed to? Why this?" Maxwell paced back and forth in his bedroom. Beads of sweat formed across his forehead. "I can't believe this," he continued to say.

He picked up the phone to dial Lina's number. Holding the phone in his hand, he stared at the screen. "No, I'm not going to call her. I can't call her. No wonder she was so sick. It probably wasn't a cold at all. Maybe it was something worse. And to think I was over there." Maxwell spewed words like venom. "I was around her. I let her hug me. I let her kiss me on my cheek. I ate off her dishes. I drank out of her glasses. How dare she do this to me?" Maxwell was furious. "I'm going to get to the bottom of this. This ain't over, Lina," he threatened. "There is no way this is over."

****

Several days passed. Lina was feeling much better. She was getting out of the house more, and she was beginning to feel more like herself. She hadn't heard from Maxwell, and dared not to call him. She wanted to give him time to process everything. Unsure of how he would react, fear gripped her heart.

Why does my life have to be as it is? she thought. Sadness overshadowed her. *Why did I have to be the one to contract this horrible disease? There are women and girls out there who are promiscuous. They use their bodies like its nothing, yet they remain clean. But I had to get this.* Of all the counseling she had, and out of all the support groups she joined, none of them could answer that question for her. None of them could give her the peace she sought. Although they tried, none of them could help her understand the illness, where it originated from and why it was so aggressive and cruel. *My life is over*, she thought.

Just when my life was starting to get good, this disease has destroyed me yet again.

Cheri returned home from her convention and hurried over to visit Lina. She missed her best friend and was eager to see her. They had talked a few times since Lina got her phone back, but it wasn't the same as being in each other's presence. Cheri knocked on the door and waited for Lina to let her in.

"Hey, girl," Cheri said with excitement.

"Hey, Cheri," Lina replied dryly.

"What's wrong with you?"

"It's a long story. I don't care to go into it right now."

Cheri looked around Lina's apartment. "Girl, it looks so gloomy in here. That cold must have really been kicking your butt, because you never let your apartment look like this. What have you been doing?" Papers were strolled across the desk and floor. Photo proofs were lying all over the desk, and dishes were in the sink.

"I've been working, trying to get back into the groove of things. That's all. You'll have to excuse my mess today."

"Girl, please," Cheri countered. "Let me help you get this stuff up." Cheri immediately started helping Lina clean. She felt bad about not being there while Lina was sick. The least she could do was to help her get organized again.

"So, what's been going on?" Cheri asked, after she and Lina settled in on the couch.

"Not much. Trying to get back into the swing of things," Lina replied.

"I understand. It's going to take time." Changing the subject, Cheri asked, "And Maxwell? How is he?"

"I haven't talked to him in a few days. I'm guessing he's okay." Lina failed to show the excitement she normally displayed when speaking about him.

"Did something happen between you two?"

"No, not really. It's a long story."

"I've got time?"

"Well, I'm not ready to tell it," Lina snapped.

"Uh, okay. That's all right. I guess I'll leave that alone." Cheri shot back.

"Yeah, let's just leave it alone," Lina agreed.

"Are you going to church tomorrow?" Cheri asked. She hoped her question would give her a clue as to how drastic the issue between Maxwell and Lina was.

"Yeah, I'm going. Why wouldn't I?"

"I figured since there's an issue going on between you and Maxwell you wouldn't want to go."

"Cheri, I've told you from the beginning. I didn't go to church for him, or any other man for that matter. That's still the case. I enjoy hearing Pastor James deliver the message, and I enjoy the choir singing. That's why I've been going and that is why I'll continue to go."

"I hear you, girl," Cheri relented. "I sure ain't about to let a man run me out of church either."

"Can we please change the subject?" Lina pleaded. "Tell me about your trip."

Cheri filled Lina in on the details of her convention. She shared with her the details of the hotel she stayed at, the meals she ate, and the meetings she took part in.

"Girl, it was work, work, work," Cheri said. "I'm so glad to be home."

Lina reached out and hugged her friend. "I'm glad you're home too."

Chapter 32

"Good morning, Minister Lee," Sister Charlotte greeted. Her smile was as big as ever. "I'm glad to see you."

"Thanks, Sister Charlotte."

Charlotte looked at Maxwell. She could tell something was troubling him, but she didn't know what. "Hmm, I wonder what's eating him," she said to Deacon Murray.

"Who knows about these young kids, Charlotte?" Deacon Murray replied.

Pastor James entered the church behind Maxwell. "Good morning, Minister Lee."

"Good morning, Pastor. How are you?"

"Oh, I'm blessed, son. I'm blessed." Pastor James paused, recalling a thought. "Minister, I want you to deliver the prayer and scripture this morning before I get up before the people. I was going to have Minister Felix to do it, but his wife has taken ill, and he won't be here this morning. So, if you'll do that for me, I'd appreciate it."

"I'm sorry, Pastor, I can't today." Maxwell stood with his eyes downcast.

"What do you mean by you can't today?" Pastor James couldn't believe what he was hearing. "Now, Minister, the Bible tells us to be ready at all times. The Word of God says to be instant in season and out of season."

"Pastor, I mean no disrespect. I know what the Word says, but please excuse me this morning. I don't feel much up to praying or reading the scriptures."

"Son, it ain't about how you feel. How are you going to take over as pastor leading the flock when you can't even pray when you're going through? What's going on with you?"

"Pastor, you have to preach this morning. I don't want to burden you with my troubles. We'll talk later."

"All right, Minister. I won't press you, but believe me, son, we will talk."

"Yes, sir, Pastor." Maxwell dropped his head, and continued to the sanctuary taking his usual seat in the pulpit.

Lina quietly entered the sanctuary wearing a pink, cowl neck dress. She took a seat towards the back of the church. She sat off to the side, hoping she would not be in Maxwell's direct view. It was hard enough looking at him in the pulpit knowing what had transpired. She couldn't imagine sitting through the entire service having him stare at her. Holding her head down, she quietly prayed. *Lord, give me strength.*

"Hey, girl," Cheri called out, drawing Lina's attention. She arrived after Lina. "Look at me, now I'm the late one," she joked. "There was an accident on the Dan Ryan that slowed me up. Thank you for saving me a seat."

"No problem," Lina replied.

Lina held back tears as the youth choir belted out a song by Youthful Praise called "After This". Although it was one of her favorite songs, somehow she was having a hard time believing the words of the song at that moment.

"There will be glory after this," The choir rang out with exhilaration.

Normally, Lina would be on her feet clapping and swaying, but this time she remained seated. *Will there, Lord? Will there be glory for me after this?* She prayed within herself.

The choir continued, *"God's gonna turn it around. He will*

bring you out. There will be glory after this." The choir sang and sang.

"Tears welled up in Lina's eyes. *Even for me Lord. Will you turn it around for me?* she prayed.

Pastor James approached the podium. The older gentlemen moved much slower than he normally did. "Good morning, family," he said to a full congregation. "What an awesome God we serve. If you believe it, give the Lord some praise on this morning."

The sound of handclaps, Amen's and praise the Lord's filled the sanctuary. Pastor James waved his hands in the air in a show of praise. Once the sound of praises softened, Pastor James spoke. "Children of God, standing here today I can look out over the congregation and see all of your lovely faces. I see joy on some of your faces. Others of you show contentment. Some of you show peace, and then there are those that show discouragement and distraction." Pastor James scanned the audience.

"People of God, I come to remind you today that God loves you. He has your best interest at heart, and he is looking out for your good." Reaching down, Pastor James opened his Bible to the location of his bookmark. "If you would turn with me to the book of Galatians, chapter six, verses nine and ten." He paused allowing the congregation time to locate the scriptures. When the shuffling died down, he continued. "Let us read together."

The congregation stood and read in unison. *And let us not be weary in well doing: for in due season we shall reap, if we faint not. As we have therefore opportunity, let us do good unto all men, especially unto them who are of the household of faith.*

"You all may be seated," he instructed. "The word of God tells us to not be weary. Oh, don't get me wrong," he stressed. In this day and time that we are living in, we're going to face some adverse situations. Some of those things we face will rock us to our very core. Some situations will make us feel like we can't go on. They'll make us feel as though life for us as we know it has ended." Members of the congregation nodded their heads in agreement. "Some things will trick us into believing God is never going to bless us, or that He will never free us from that particular situation."

"Oh, but I'm so glad to know that the God we serve is the same God yesterday, today, and He will continue to be the same God forever." Pastor James' voice elevated with excitement. His energy appeared to increase as he paced the length of the pulpit. "When you woke up this morning, he was the same God. When you went to bed last night, he was the same God. If you're blessed to see the sunshine on tomorrow, He'll yet be the same God. You may ask what does that mean, Pastor. Well, I'm here to tell you, that means the same God that made a way for you last time will make a way for you this time. Glory to God."

Calming down, Pastor James wiped his forehead with a handkerchief. "You may look at me and think within yourself it's easy for me to make these claims because everything is going well for me. That couldn't be further from the truth. I have simply come to the realization that I serve a God that can do anything but fail. Children of God, some of you are sick in your bodies. You've been to the doctors and they couldn't fix it. You've cried, and you've prayed, and yet you continue to suffer. You don't believe you'll ever get healed, or that you will ever overcome this sickness or disease. I want to encourage you today. The same God that healed the lepers can also free you from every affliction in your body. And if He doesn't see fit to heal you, it's not because He can't." Softening his tone, he continued. "Some things, God allows us to go through so that we will trust in Him. The doctor may tell you, you only have six weeks to live, and God will give you ten years. It's because His grace is sufficient."

Stepping back behind the podium, Pastor James concluded his message. "Children of God, don't be weary when you're doing what you know is right. Even if you can't see it right now, please know God has not forgotten you. He cares for you, and He will bless you. Continue to love in spite of. Love through the hurt, love through the pain, love when it's easy, and love when it's hard. Above all else, children of God, don't give up. Better days are ahead. Concluding his sermon, Pastor James offered up a prayer for the entire congregation.

Service ended, adding a sense of relief to Lina. It was difficult for her watching Maxwell, seeing the sadness on his face and knowing she was the cause of it. She gathered her belongings and stepped out from the pew.

"Lina." Maxwell called her name, startling her. She didn't see him approaching.

"Hi, Maxwell," she replied, forcing a smile.

"I need to talk to you," he stated firmly.

Cheri looked back and forth between Maxwell and Lina. The tension between them was obvious. She focused her attention on Lina, offering her a way out.

Shyly, Lina replied, "That'll be fine. Where do you want to talk?"

"Come with me." Maxwell walked Lina to her car. The parking lot was beginning to clear out. "Lina, why didn't you tell me?" he asked angrily. He was trying to remain calm as he questioned her. He didn't want to make a scene at the church.

Lina could see the anger etched across his forehead. Afraid of where the conversation was going, she asked, "Maxwell, can you come by my apartment so that we can talk. I don't want to go into this out here. Please, give me a chance to explain."

"No, I don't think that's a good idea. I don't need to be at your apartment right now. Why didn't you tell me?" Maxwell continued in spite of Lina's objections. "You knew I had developed feelings for you. I thought we were headed towards something, and now this. How do you expect me to get past all of this? It's too much to deal with, Lina. I deserve better than this."

Lina grew tired of Maxwell's attack. If he was going to take it there, she was going to go there with him. "Wait a minute. You deserve better than what? It's not like we were a couple, Maxwell. Yes, we've spent time together and we've enjoyed each other's company, but I had no commitments to you, and you had no commitments to me. Why would I disclose such a thing? For you to attack me the way you're doing now?" she asked. "We weren't having an intimate relationship. That's where it matters most. You can't get it from being in my presence, Maxwell. It's not airborne."

Her frustrations mounted. "I'm not going to sit here and let you talk down to me. Nor will I allow you to belittle me. Realize something, Maxwell, this is something that was given to me. It's not something I acquired at random. I didn't pick it up at the grocery store. If you would allow me to explain the situation to you, you might actually understand. But not like this.

"You kissed me," he yelled.

"On the jaw," Lina retorted. Maxwell, I kissed your jaw. You would be the first man in history to get it from a kiss on the jaw. We didn't exchange bodily fluids, if you'll recall. As a matter of fact, while you're going off on me, when was the last time you checked your status." Exhausted, Lina said, "I don't have to put up with this. If you'll excuse me, please." Lina pushed past Maxwell and got into her car. She pulled away leaving him standing in the parking lot looking dazed.

"Maxwell, you are going to tell me what's going on," Cheri demanded, approaching him from behind. "I've never seen her this upset. What did you do to her?"

"What did I do to her?" he barked back.

"That's what I said. She's clearly upset because of you."

Shifting his stance, he said. "You don't know, do you?"

"Know what?"

Laughing wickedly, he repeated. "Oh my God, you don't know. I'll tell you what, why don't you go and ask your friend why I'm so upset. Maybe she'll give you the answers that she won't give me." Maxwell stormed away.

"What is all of this commotion out here?" Pastor James stepped out from the church. Seeing Maxwell marching away from Cheri, he commanded his attention. "Minister Lee, come with me. I want to talk to you."

Pastor James escorted Maxwell to his office. "Now, son, I know we're only human and we're yet in the flesh. The Bible says be ye angry and sin not. You looked like you were getting pretty close to sinning out here. What's going on?"

"It's, Lina, Pastor," he explained. "What she did to me was cruel." Anger filled Maxwell's heart.

"What did she do?" Pastor James asked calmly.

"I found out something about her that she could have told me, Pastor, but she didn't. I had to find out on my own. It's worse than I could have ever imagined."

"That sweet young girl?" Pastor James asked in disbelief. What in the world could she have done?"

Maxwell took a deep breath, but said nothing. Although he was angry, he didn't feel right about sharing Lina's condition.

Pastor James sensed his reserve. "Minister, anything you said to me is kept in confidence. I won't share it with anyone. That's part of the oath I took. You can trust me. Now tell me, son, what happened?"

Feeling more relaxed, Maxwell spoke freely. "Lina and I have been spending a lot of time together. I developed some strong feelings for her. In fact, I was falling in love with her. We never did anything inappropriate, and we were never intimate or anything like that, but we became very close." Maxwell sat back in the chair and continued to speak. "Last week she got sick. I went by to check on her, and I helped take care of her. While I was there, I went into the restroom. There was a bottle of medication on the sink."

"You looked at her medication?" Pastor James interrupted.

"No, Pastor, it wasn't anything like that. When I went to wash my hands, I knocked it off. Once I picked it up, I noticed the name of it. I didn't think anything of it, because I thought it was allergy medicine. It wasn't until I was listening to the news the next morning that I found out the medicine was actually HIV medication. She knew how close we were getting, Pastor, but she didn't tell me she had HIV. She could have told me she had AIDS."

"AIDS or HIV, son? You know there is a difference."

"There's no difference. It's the same thing."

"No, there is a difference." Pastor James confirmed. Continuing, he asked. "Did you give her a chance to explain?"

"Yeah, that's what our conversation outside was all about. I asked her why she didn't tell me," Maxwell's voice became elevated.

"What did she say to you?"

"She told me to come by her house so that she could explain. She didn't want to go into it out here."

"Well, whether it was her house or some other location, I will agree the church grounds was not the appropriate place for it."

Becoming frustrated, Maxwell forced air out of his teeth. "Why do I have to be the bad guy? Why does it all have to fall on me? Why are you making me out to be the one that's wrong in this situation?"

"Slow down, son. I know you're upset, but remember where you are. I didn't say you were the one that was wrong. I'm not taking anyone's side." Looking Maxwell squarely in the eyes, Pastor James asked, "Son, have you prayed about this? Did you pray before you approached her?"

"What good is that going to do?" Maxwell yelped.

Pastor James quoted Proverbs chapter three verse six. "In all thy ways acknowledge Him. He will direct your path." Rising from behind the desk, he opened the door for Maxwell to leave. "It's time you started praying, son."

"I have prayed, and look where it's gotten me." Maxwell stormed out of the Pastor's office. He pulled his phone out of his pocket and immediately deleted Lina's number. *They want to pray so bad, let them pray for her, she's the one that needs it. I'm good.*

Chapter 33

Tears filled Lina's eyes as she drove down the street. She expected it to be difficult when Maxwell confronted her, but that was too much. He talked to her like she was his enemy. Maxwell's reaction reminded her of why she didn't allow people, especially men, to get close to her. Lina could still see the anger in his eyes and feel the sting of his words on her ears. *And he calls himself a minister,* she thought. *Ministers were supposed to be more Christ-like than anybody.* A small part of her wanted to sympathize with him. She understood his being angry, but the way he handled it was completely uncalled for.

Lina arrived at her apartment and slammed the door closed. Her throat felt dry and scratchy. She went into the kitchen and poured herself a glass of water. Leaning on the counter, she wiped the tears from her eyes as they fell. The doorbell rang, startling her. *Don't tell me he followed me home,* she thought. She remained still, hoping if it was Maxwell, he would go away.

"It's me, Lina. Open up," Cheri yelled from the other side of the door. The doorbell continued to ring.

Placing her cup on the counter, Lina wiped her eyes and walked over to the door. "Here I come," she yelled, hoping to stop Cheri from ringing the doorbell. She opened the door and allowed Cheri to enter.

"What happened at the church today?" Cheri asked. Concern riddled her voice.

Lina took a seat on the couch. "I don't want to talk about

it," Lina cried.

"I know you're upset, but you're going to have to tell me something. I can't let it go that easy. After you left, I asked Maxwell what his problem was. I wanted to know why he was treating you like that. He said I needed to ask you. So I'm asking. What is he talking about, Lina?"

Tired of living in secret, Lina took a deep breath and explained to Cheri what happened. She looked up at Cheri and offered her a seat on the couch. "You're gonna want to sit down for this."

Cheri complied. "Lina, you're scaring me."

"It's nothing to be scared of. Although I don't know how you'll take it." Lina took a deep breath. "Cheri, I have HIV." Lina allowed Cheri to process what she told her.

"What," she exclaimed. "How? When? Why didn't you tell me? Oh, my God, Lina." Cheri jumped up from the couch and paced the floor. She sat, then she stood, then she sat again. She wasn't mentally prepared for the news Lina had given her. She was expecting Lina to tell her she had met another guy and Maxwell found out. Cheri was in a daze. The moment seemed surreal. Collecting herself, Cheri moved back over to the couch next to Lina. After the way Maxwell had treated her friend earlier, she figured she owed it to her to show compassion. "How did this happen, Lina? When did you find out?" she asked with concern.

Lina was surprised by Cheri's reaction. She expected her reaction to be similar to Maxwell's. She was relieved. Lina thought back to the day her life changed forever. She turned towards her friend and shared the story with her.

"It started when I was in college. I was always a homebody, so I didn't really date much in high school. I had always wanted to attend Duke University. Even though I lived in Durham, I chose to stay in the dorms on campus. My dorm was co-ed. At first my parents were totally against it, but after they were given the dorm specifications and rules they agreed to let me live there."

"That's where I met Kaine. He was so fine, Cheri. He was athletic, and well known on campus. He had the blackest, naturally curly hair I had ever seen. He had a way with words too. He made me feel like I was the best woman in the world. We flirted back and forth for a while before I agreed to go out with him. Because of my lack of experience, I wanted to take things extra slow. He went along with it for a while, and we developed a pretty good relationship." Lina smiled through her reflections.

Cheri clung to every word. "Kaine knew I was a virgin. The fact that he didn't pressure me attracted me even more. He had met my family and even attended family functions with me. All around campus, I was known as Kaine's girl. It didn't bother me because Kaine had a great reputation. I was hated among a lot of the women on campus, but in the circles he ran in, I was pretty much accepted."

"So, let me get this straight," Cheri interrupted. This Kaine guy was your first boyfriend? Dang, girl, what were you? A hermit?"

"No, I was not a hermit. I was pretty shy, but more than that, I wasn't about no mess. In high school, there were a lot of messy guys. I saw girls have their reputations destroyed by these guys. I wasn't trying to go there, so I figured the best way to keep it from happening to me was to keep to myself. Don't get me wrong, my decision didn't come without consequences. I can't tell you how many times I was accused of being gay."

"Okay, I didn't mean to interrupt. Go ahead with your story."

Lina thought back to where she had left off. "So, like I said, we had been together over a year, and we hadn't been intimate. One night, Kaine was in my dorm room pretty late. My roommate was out for the night, and we were studying. He decided he wanted to get frisky. I knew I wouldn't be able to keep him off for much longer, so I gave in. He used a condom, but it broke. I was mortified. The first thing I thought was I could be pregnant. I was nervous for weeks." Lina laughed at her reflection. "Girl, I took at least ten pregnancy tests. When he approached me again sexually, I told him I didn't want to go there. I couldn't take a chance on ending up pregnant. By the third no, Kaine was pretty much fed up. Shortly after, he broke up with me."

"That's all fine and well, but you still haven't told me how you found out you were infected."

"I'm getting to it," she replied. "My roommate and I were taking a health class together and the instructor covered a chapter on infectious disease. He encouraged the students to get tested for HIV. He stressed the importance of knowing your status. She and I went together to get tested. Needless to say, my results came back Positive. I knew exactly where I had gotten it, because Kaine was the only guy I had ever been with. He was my first, and my last."

Silence filled the room like a thick cloud. Cheri didn't know what to say. HIV always seemed like a distant disease that only happened to bad people. She always thought people that got HIV were homosexual men, drug addicts, and women that abused their bodies. Listening to Lina's story, she realized how wrong she had been. She thought about her unprotected exploits. She was no different from Lina. She had put herself at risk as much as anyone else had. For the first time, she considered getting tested.

"What happened to Kaine?" Cheri asked.

"It's funny you should ask that. When I went home a couple of months ago for my father's birthday, my cousin told me Kaine had been killed. He knew he was infected, yet he continued to sleep with women unprotected. He also didn't share his status with them. Apparently, one of his victims took his life."

"Wow, that's deep." Cheri sat in disbelief. She had no idea Lina had endured so much. Compassion filled her heart.

Cheri hugged her friend, and allowed her to cry on her shoulders. Rubbing her hair she asked, "Why was Maxwell so upset?"

"He was mad because I didn't tell him," Lina uttered between sobs.

"If you didn't tell him, how did he find out?"

"The day he came over when I was sick, he saw my medicine on the bathroom counter." Lina set up and faced her friend. "Maxwell is the first guy I have been interested in since Kaine. I was going to tell him, but I was waiting to see if the relationship was going somewhere first. I don't just go around telling everybody my status."

"I understand," Cheri said, placing her hands on top of Lina's. "I'm sure if it was me, I would have done the same thing you did. But Lina, why didn't you tell me."

"I didn't want to lose your friendship."

"Girlfriend, I'm not going anywhere. You're my friend and if nobody sticks by you, I will."

Relief filled Lina's heart. After hiding for so long, she finally felt free. Cheri's reaction gave her hope. Although she wasn't ready to go public with her status, it helped knowing those closest to her knew the truth. Knowing the truth gave both Cheri and Maxwell the option either to accept her as she was, or to leave her life permanently. Either way, she knew she would be ok.

"Lina," Cheri said. "I'm sorry about Maxwell. I know you and he were getting pretty close. I could tell he made you happy. To be honest with you, you made him pretty happy too. I never told you this, but Maxwell became a different person after he met you. He had always been friendly, but he seemed like he laughed more. When you were sick, and I couldn't get in touch with you, he rushed over here to check on you. I know he's upset right now, but I still believe he's in love with you." Cheri grabbed Lina's hand. "I know it seems bad right now, but if it's meant to be, it'll be in spite of this."

"Thanks, Cheri," Lina said as fresh tears fell.

Chapter 34

Maxwell set quietly in his office, sulking. He avoided the sales floor as much as possible. A tap on the door drew his attention. "Come in," he said without identifying the visitor.

Maxine entered the office carrying a bag of food. She had stopped by a restaurant on the way to the store. She made her way inside and stood in front of his desk. "Since you always seem to find a way to get out of going out to eat with me, I decided to bring lunch to you. I have an armed guard stationed outside the door so you can't run."

Maxwell laughed. Maxine's unexpected gesture lightened his mood. "In that case, let me see what you got. Maxwell beckoned for Maxine to take a seat. She gladly complied. He saw a difference in Maxine that day. Although she was extremely beautiful, she was dressed more modestly. She wore a pair of dark blue fitted jeans, a black V-neck BeBe t-shirt, and black Jimmy Choo peep-toe pumps.

"Look what I brought," she said with delight. "I stopped by Nicky's Restaurant on my way over here and got you a Big Baby with grilled onions and fries. I got me a pizza puff and fries. That place still looks the same after all these years."

A huge smile displayed on Maxwell's lips. "I haven't had one of these bad boys in years. Aw, man, I'm gonna devour this." Maxwell looked at the succulent, double cheeseburger like it was the best thing on earth. He turned around and retrieved two soft drinks from the dorm-sized refrigerator he kept in his office.

Maxine didn't know what triggered the change in Maxwell but she was glad something had. She intended to take full advantage of his sudden change of heart. It was more important than ever for her to secure him as her man, because her coworkers were starting to suspect her and Jonathan Freeman of being involved. Seeing her out with Maxwell would derail their thoughts. All she needed was for a few select gossipers to see them out together and it would seal the deal. She tried to stay in the loop at work as much as possible in order to keep up with everyone's whereabouts. Knowing where they were going, gave her insight on the places she and Jonathan needed to avoid. Jonathan was aware of her scheme, but cautioned her to keep things at a safe distance. After all, she was his woman, and he wasn't going to give her up. As long as Jonathan continued to support her the way he did, he didn't have to worry about her going anywhere.

She knew Maxwell would never be able to support her the way Jonathan did. Although Maxwell lived well for his financial bracket, she was on another level. She paid more for her handbags than he charged for his best suits. Not to mention his little Cadillac Escalade. It was peanuts compared to her car. She figured the average person would think he was balling, but in her world, he wasn't even on the court.

Picking up his burger, Maxwell took a huge bite. "Mmm, this is just how I remember it. Thank you, Maxine."

"You're welcome. I'm glad you like it." Maxine on the other hand struggled with her meal. It had been a long time since she had eaten the processed, greasy, meat pastry. In order to keep her fingers and her clothes from becoming an unsightly mess, she opted to use a plastic fork she picked up at the restaurant.

Maxwell noticed her efforts and laughed. "You mean to tell me you're that uppity that you have to eat your pizza puff with a fork."

"Forget you, Maxwell. I'm not uppity. I have somewhere to go after this, and I don't want to get my clothes messed up. Leave me alone," she replied joining him in laughter.

The two shared easy conversation as they ate. Maxwell shared with her his desire to expand his business to other parts of the city. He also talked to her about his ministry goals. Maxine told him about her law school experiences and the difficulty of the bar exam. Of course, she made herself look good by telling him she passed with flying colors on her first try. She knew Maxwell would never check her facts, so she was able to make her story as elaborate as she wanted.

After spending two hours together, Maxine got up to leave. She didn't want to wear out her welcome, especially since Maxwell was starting to come around. Maxwell came from around the desk and gave her a hug. The sweet scent of her perfume played in his nostrils. *One way or another he was going to get over Lina*, he thought. If Maxine was the way to get it done, then so be it.

Opening the door for her, he said, "I'm so rude. How is your mother doing?"

"What?" Maxine asked completely oblivious to previous lies about her mother.

"Your mother, Ms. Miller, how is she? I failed to ask you about her condition. Is she continuing to improve?"

"Oh, I don't know where my mind is. You must have mesmerized me with those muscles," she teased. "Mama is doing much better. It was touch and go for a while, but the doctors expect her to make a full recovery." Glancing at her watch, she said, "Oh, my goodness I should have been out of here. I have an appointment I have to get to." Maxine kissed Maxwell on the cheek and headed out the door.

"Thanks for coming by," he said. He stared at her until she disappeared out of his sight. *If you can't beat them, you may as well join them.*

Chapter 35

Things were starting to get back on track for Lina. She poured herself into her work more than ever before. When she wasn't doing photo shoots for clients, she was building her portfolio with stock photos she had taken. Her photos from the Children's Museum gained notoriety, and opened the door for more requests from public arenas. The pay was significant. She used some of the money to update her photography equipment. She put the rest in savings.

She no longer felt comfortable attending Christ the True Vine Church. She opted to visit various churches instead. She was confident she would find one to attend on a regular basis. She missed the choir, and hearing Pastor James deliver the message, but she knew along with those things came Maxwell.

Her revelation caused Cheri to take a look at herself and to reconsider her actions. With Lina's support, she decided to get tested for HIV. Lina met Cheri at the doctor's office and waited with her for the results. Lina made small talk to keep Cheri calm while they waited on the doctor to enter the room.

A young African American woman with short dreadlocks entered the room carrying a tablet computer. The doctor's office had recently updated their process, and patient records were filed electronically. After shaking each of the women's hands, the doctor commended Cheri on her decision to be tested.

"It always pleases me to see young ladies make the bold move to have this test done. There are so many individuals walking around infected unknowingly. The fact that you're here tells me that you are not only concerned about your own health, but the health of others as well. I wish more people would take the step that you have taken. Many of the people that choose not to be tested do so because they are afraid of the results. They fail to realize if they test positive, prompt treatment will be to their benefit. There have been many advances in the treatment of HIV. Although there is still no cure, people are living longer, healthier lives with the help of routine medications. Before we continue on to the results, I have to ask if you would like for your friend to leave the room."

"No, I want her in here. Please go ahead."

The doctor smiled tenderly. "All right, now that we have that out of the way, let's get to your results." Using her finger, the doctor made a few short taps on her tablet. "Here we are." Looking up at Cheri, she smiled. "Cheri, your results are negative."

"Oh, thank God," Cheri declared. She exhaled deeply, expelling air she didn't realize she was holding.

"Now, Cheri, although your results are negative, you still need to continue to make sound decisions and protect yourself if you find yourself in an at risk situation."

"Thank you doctor." Cheri and Lina stood to leave. "And don't worry, I'll be careful. I view life much differently these days."

Cheri and Lina decided to have lunch after leaving the doctor's office. "I'm happy for you, Cheri. I know those were the scariest minutes of your life." Lina smiled at her friend. "I'm also genuinely proud of you. When you found out about me, you could have easily turned your back on me. You chose to remain my friend, and you still treat me the same as you did before you found out. That means the most to me."

"You know I love you, girl. You're my best friend, and I'm

not going to let your illness stop that. In my opinion, it's no different than if you had cancer, or lupus, or something else. To be honest with you, it upsets me. When someone is diagnosed with cancer or something like that, people want to rally and throw benefits and everything. But when you hear someone tested positive for HIV or has AIDS people treat them like they're dirty and nasty. It's not right. Your trust in the man you were in love with got you in this situation. Nothing more, nothing less."

Lina's expression grew solemn. "Cheri, I know I appear to be strong, but to be honest with you, I have a lot of weak moments. I mean, I'm a young woman. I desire to get married one day. I know I'll never have children of my own, but I would like to have a family at some point in my life. In some of the support groups I'm affiliated with, I hear stories of HIV-Negative people choosing to remain with and even marry their HIV-Positive companions. I guess a big part of me thought Maxwell would be that person for me. That's why I opened up and allowed him to get close to me."

Cheri hated to see her friend so upset. "I understand, Lina. Do you remember the last time you attended church with me?"

"How could I forget?" Lina replied, sadly.

"I'm not talking about that part. Besides the drama Maxwell brought, do you remember the service?"

"Vaguely," she replied.

"Well, I can't forget it. In fact it keeps me going." Cheri smiled at her reflections. "Pastor James preached the sermon about not being weary when things don't go our way, because God is the same God yesterday, today, and forever."

"I'm sure you're going somewhere with this, right Cheri."

"Yes I am. Now listen," she challenged. "You said in your meetings you hear stories of how some of the people that are infected end up in happy, productive relationships. Now whether or not the person for you will be HIV positive or negative I cannot say, but I can remind you of God's love for you and his promise to give you the desires of your heart. Since He is the same God, He will bless you the same way He blessed those other people."

Lina considered her words. It must have been a God thing because she took comfort in Cheri's words. Instead of remaining down, she felt lifted and encouraged. She began to think back to the sermon Cheri was referring to. Slowly the words of the song, "After This" played in her mind.

There will be glory after this. There will be victory after this. God will turn it around. He will bring you out. There will be glory after this.

Chapter 36

"What's up, baby bruh?" Jason's excitement penetrated the phone line.

"Hey, Jason man. What's going on? You sound like you're jumping up and down over there. Let me guess; you've met some new honey and you can't wait to tell me about her."

"Man, that's foul. Why does it have to be a woman making me happy? I do have other things going on in my life, even though you and Mama refuse to acknowledge it."

"My bad, man. I didn't mean to bring you down. What's up with you?"

"That's more like it. I just called to tell you the deal is done. I got the keys, man."

Maxwell was somewhat confused. He knew he had been a bit distracted since he started spending time with Maxine, but he couldn't recall Jason telling him about a deal he was working on. "What did you do, get a new ride."

"Naw, man, it's much bigger than that. I just closed on my house. Holla at ya boy."

"What?" Maxwell shouted. "Man, you're lying. For real? You bought a house. Where at?"

"Yeah, man. I'm serious as a heart attack. It's over on 65th and Rockwell."

"Aw, man. I'm happy for you. Dude, how'd you pull that off? Have you told Mama?"

"Slow down, Max, man. How many questions are you going to hit me with at once? I feel like I'm being interrogated or something." Jason laughed at his own pun. "I did it by working hard. All those times when you and Mama was thinking I was laying around wasting my life, I was out working my butt off. All my stuff is legit. Shoot, half the time when y'all couldn't get in touch with me, I was either at work or somewhere sleep because I had just gotten off work."

"But, man, what about all of those raggedy apartments you were staying in?"

"Dude, the rent was cheap. I was trying to save up for my own crib. I knew I wasn't going to be there long anyway. I just needed a place to lay my head when I got off work."

"Mama is going to be so proud of you. Have you told her yet?"

"Will you stop asking me that?" Jason grew agitated. "I haven't talked to Mama. She ain't ever been proud of me before. I don't know why she would start now. All my life she has been telling me I wasn't going to be nothing because my daddy wasn't nothing in her eyes. After I got older, and left home, I wasn't trying to hear that mess. I found my daddy and started visiting him in prison. The more she told me I wouldn't be anything because of him, the more he told me to be better than him. He was actually the one that encouraged me to work for what I wanted, and not to take the easy way out like he did hustling. I can't tell you how many times I heard him say, 'You see where hustling got me. I better not see you up in here.' I followed his advice and that's why I'm doing it big, bruh."

"Dang, man. I guess there's a lot I didn't know."

"It's all good," Jason laughed. "Now, when can you come and help me move in? I got some stuff that needs to be put together, and it requires two people."

"Man, just tell me when and I'll be there."

"Bet."

Maxwell ended his call with Jason and sat dazed. In some ways he had treated his brother the same way their mother had. They both had chosen to look at the outside and judged Jason according to what they perceived, rather than finding out what was really going on in his life. He felt there was some lesson he was supposed to be learning that he wasn't getting. Only time would tell.

Chapter 37

Things between Maxine and Maxwell were progressing faster than she had expected. She wanted to keep him close, but she couldn't allow him to be overpowering. She had to admit she enjoyed his company, but he would never be on her level. She had a certain standard, and no matter what he did, there was no way he would ever measure up.

Maxine was confident she would get everything from Maxwell she desired. She knew she had gotten to him when he shared with her the details of why he and Lina stopped communicating. *That was messed up*, she thought. Finding out Lina had HIV had to be devastating. She would never be in that situation. If she had HIV it would just have to take her out because that was one test she was determined to never take. She would not be the one sitting in a doctor's office somewhere receiving that kind of news. She knew if people could read her mind, they would probably think she was a terrible person. In her opinion, if she got HIV, it would be because someone gave it to her, and if she passed it on to someone else, oh well.

The time she spent with Maxwell and Jonathan too, for that matter, was simply a means to an end. Jonathan provided the lifestyle to which she had become accustomed, and Maxwell kept the attention off her and Jonathan. Her plan to have her coworkers see her and Maxwell out together was working its magic. They were even starting to ask her questions about Maxwell when she went to work. Jonathan was free to send her flowers and other items to the office because everyone assumed they were from Maxwell.

Jonathan was secure in his relationship with Maxine. She kept him informed about her dealings with Maxwell. One thing was for sure, she wasn't going to allow Maxwell to mess with her money. She and Maxwell would always meet in public places. They frequented restaurants and theaters. She didn't allow him to visit her apartment, using his status as a minister as the excuse. The reality was she refused to put in the effort to conceal photos she had of Jonathan displayed throughout the apartment.

A few more months and she could end this façade. Her first thought was to take it all the way to the altar, but the fact that she could achieve the same results without the commitment was appealing. Stupid Maxwell, he was no different from the other nothing men she had come across. Everyone seemed to want to be in love. Please, love was overrated in her opinion. It was a dog eat dog world, and she was going to be the one doing the eating.

Chapter 38

"How are things going with you, Minister? " Pastor James asked. "I haven't talked with you in a while."

"Pastor, what do you mean? We talked the other day in Bible Study."

"You know that's not what I'm talking about, son." Pastor James eyed Maxwell suspiciously. "I'm not referring to our conversations about church business. I'd like to know what's going on in your life."

"Well, Pastor, you told me I needed a helpmate, so I'm working on making that happen."

"Oh," Pastor James replied with more of a statement than a response.

Maxwell looked hard at Pastor James. "What is that supposed to mean, Pastor?"

"Son, have you prayed about it?"

"Why do you always ask me that, Pastor? Of course, I prayed." Maxwell was struggling to maintain his composure. He respected Pastor James but lately the old man seemed to think he was more Maxwell's father than he was his pastor. Maxwell wanted to follow in his footsteps and succeed him as pastor, but he wasn't going to allow Pastor James to put him under a microscope.

"Son, in all that you do, make sure you are being led by the Spirit of God. Whoever that helpmate is you're working on, make sure she is of God. We can get ourselves into some horrible messes when we leave God out of things." Lately talking to Maxwell was like talking to a wall. Nothing Pastor James said to him seemed to get through.

"Pastor James, you don't have to worry about me. I'm good. I'll still be able to step in when you retire and take this ministry to the place God has destined for it to go." On that note, Maxwell headed home.

Maxwell couldn't shake his conversation with Pastor James. It seemed lately there was no pleasing him. Maxwell was okay with the way things were going with him and Maxine. He would only admit to himself the fact that he didn't like the way she viewed money. They had been out several times, but it was always to expensive restaurants or theaters. If he suggested getting pizza, she'd whisk him off to an Italian restaurant. If he mentioned a burger, they ended up at one of Chicago's most expensive steak houses. When he wanted to see a movie, she had him going to an Opera or some other theater production. She was working a number on his bank account. He didn't want her to think he couldn't provide for her if he became her husband, so he continued on.

The phone rang pulling him back to the present. Pushing the button on his hands free device he answered. "Hello."

"What's up, Max," his brother announced.

"Hey, Jason. What's up, man?" Maxwell made a left turn and drove in the direction of his townhouse.

"Remember when I said I was going to need your help over at my house?" Jason paused and waited for Maxwell's response. "Today is the day. I know you should be out of church by now. Can you come by here?"

"Yeah, I can come and help you. Give me time to get home to change clothes and grab a bite to eat and I'll be over there."

"All right, bet." Jason replied. "Do you want me to go ahead and give you the address now?"

"No, I'll get it when I'm on my way. If you give it to me now I'll forget it."

"Ok, cool. I'll see you in a few."

Maxwell still found it hard to believe Jason had accomplished such a feat. Had Jason not told him directly, there was no way he would have believed it coming from anyone else. However, he didn't agree with Jason's decision to keep his news from their mother. He realized Jason and his mother didn't have the best relationship, but it was time they ironed out their differences.

Activating the voice dial feature on his phone, Maxwell placed a call to his mother. Marilyn answered the call after the second ring. "Hey, Ma. How are you making it?"

"I'm doing good, baby. How are you doing?"

"I'm all right. I was calling to see what you had planned this afternoon."

"Nothing really. I'm getting ready to cook. I was going to call you and Jason to see if y'all wanted to come by and eat. I haven't seen either one of you in a while now."

"Sounds like I caught you just in time. Tell you what. Don't start cooking. I'm getting ready to stop by my house, then I'm coming by there to pick you up. I want to take you somewhere."

"Okay," Marilyn replied hesitantly. "Where are we going, baby?"

"It's a surprise, so get ready."

"In that case, I'll be ready when you get here."

Maxwell chose to keep both Marilyn and Jason in the dark about their unexpected visit.

Maxwell and Marilyn pulled in front of the brick house. The realtor's for sale sign remained in the ground with a small red Sold sign posted in the corner. Marilyn looked at Maxwell confused. "Maxwell who's house is this? You know how I am about meeting new people."

A huge grin formed on Maxwell's lips. "This is Jason's house, Ma."

Marilyn wrinkled her forehead. "Jason, who?"

"Your son, Jason."

Marilyn sat quietly in shock. She wondered if Maxwell was playing a cruel joke on her. There was no way this was her son's house. "What, he finally got a woman that has some money to take care of him?"

"No, Ma. He did this on his own. Open your eyes, Ma. This should make you very proud as a mother. There's a lot you don't know about him."

Maxwell got out of the vehicle and walked around to help Marilyn out. They climbed the stairs with ease. Maxwell rang the doorbell and waited for Jason to answer.

Jason looked out the front window and saw Maxwell's truck parked in front of his house. "What's up, baby bruh," he said as he opened the door. Obvious surprise displayed on his face when he saw Marilyn standing at the door next to Maxwell.

Without a word, she reached out and held him in her arms. Tears dropped on his shirt as she laid her head on his chest. "I'm sorry, son, I'm so sorry for everything."

Jason wrapped his arms around his mother, returning her embrace. "It's ok, Ma. I forgive you. I'm sorry too."

Maxwell stood back and allowed his brother, and their mother, space to have their much needed moment.

Releasing their embrace, Jason welcomed them into his home. Following a brief tour, they went to work setting up the house. Marilyn put up decorations and set up the bedrooms while Maxwell and Jason assembled various items.

Once Marilyn finished in the bedrooms, she made her way to the kitchen. As if on cue, she prepared the first home cooked meal in her son's house.

Chapter 39

The ticket taker scanned Lina's boarding pass before directing her to the jet bridge. She boarded the plane with ease, placing her photo equipment in the overhead compartment. Settling in, she relaxed and awaited take off. The flight attendant gave Lina and the other passengers final in-flight instructions before going to her designated seat.

The roar of the engines sent nervous butterflies fluttering in Lina's belly. As many times as she had flown, she never got used to the takeoff. She gripped the armrest as the plane increased speed and ascended. She tried to focus her attention on other things, but found it difficult. In no time, the plane began to level off. Thoughts of relief swept through her mind when the seat belt sign went off.

The captain has turned off the seat belt light. You are now free to move about the cabin. The flight attendant announced.

Lina was glad the flight was only two hours and forty-five minutes long. She had never been a fan of flying, and this trip was no different. She smiled, as she reflected on the reason for her trip. She couldn't believe any day now she was going to be an aunt. Her mother had called her the previous day and told her the doctor said Zarion had dilated, and the baby was in the birth position. There was no way she was going to miss out on Daniel making his arrival. From the time Lydia told her Zarion was having a boy, Lina felt a connection to him. After ending the call with her mother, she immediately went online and booked her flight.

She wasn't sure how long she would remain in Durham, so she purchased an open ended ticket. She didn't have any appointments in the near future, so there was nothing preventing her from enjoying an extended stay. She didn't want to rush back to Chicago following Daniel's birth because she needed time to bond with him.

Lina's father met her at the airport and drove her directly to the hospital. As he drove, he filled Lina in with the details. Zarion had been at home awaiting Lina's arrival, when her water broke. Lina's brother-in-law left work and was going to meet them at the hospital.

"Daddy, are you ready to be a grandfather?" Lina asked cheerfully.

Mr. Fairweather's lips curled up into a full smile. "Yeah, baby. I'm ready. I'm looking forward to seeing my grandson."

"I know, Daddy. I'm ready too. I can't wait to hold that little man."

Lina and her father arrived at the hospital and rushed down the corridor. Zarion was in what the hospital called a labor suite. The large room was decorated in bright yellow paint with pictures of newborns placed throughout the room. A small, round table and chairs sat in one corner of the room a short distance from the bed. Two chairs sat nestled against the wall near the bed. Medical equipment and an empty bassinet sat on the opposite side of the bed.

Approaching the bed, Lina placed a kiss on Zarion's forehead. "I'm so happy for you, sis."

"Thank you, Lina. I'm glad you made it."

"Me too," Lina replied. Pulling out her camera, she took a few tasteful shots of Zarion and the labor room. Zarion didn't put up much of a fuss because her hair was styled in fresh cornrows.

Four hours later, Daniel made his arrival. Weighing in at seven pounds and eight ounces, he was a perfect little bundle of joy. Lina grabbed her camera and snapped photos to her heart's content.

Seeing her nephew's life begin gave Lina a new lease on life. She knew at that moment life was to be celebrated, not dreaded.

Chapter 40

Maxwell entered his mother's house and grabbed a cup of coffee. Marilyn had prepared breakfast for the two of them. She could tell her son had been having a tough time lately. She was determined to find out why.

He poured warm syrup over his pancakes before slicing into them. Cheesy scrambled eggs and a thick slice of ham rounded out his meal. "Ma, this food is good. You must have put your foot in it," he teased.

"Boy, you're crazy." Marilyn laughed as she watched Maxwell slowly devour his food. She could tell from his expression he was enjoying his meal.

"You will never believe who I saw the other day," she said, hoping to make small talk.

"Who?" Maxwell asked between bites.

"Rose Miller. You know, from the East Side. Remember you and Jason used to play with her daughter when you all were little. For the life of me, I can't think of her daughter's name."

"Maxine," Maxwell replied surprised.

"Yeah, that's it, Maxine." Marilyn nodded her head in agreement. Taking a sip from her coffee, she continued. "Anyway, me and a friend of mine went to eat at Red Lobster on ninety fifth and Cicero. While we were waiting to be seated, she came in with her husband. I have to give it to her, she looked good. We stood there and talked for at least thirty minutes."

Maxwell looked puzzled.

"What's wrong with you?" Marilyn asked.

"Did she mention anything about being sick?"

"No, where did you get that from? That woman was bragging about spending a month in Europe. I seriously doubt she could have been sick and in another country on vacation at the same time."

"What about Maxine? Did she say how Maxine was doing?"

"It's a shame. She said she hadn't talked to Maxine in almost a year. You know Rose always was a big talker."

"What happened between her and Maxine?" Maxwell questioned. He tried to appear oblivious to Maxine's whereabouts.

"She said they had a falling out because she didn't agree with Maxine having an affair with a married man. She said he was some big time attorney downtown. Apparently, the man bought Maxine a real expensive car, and got her an apartment in one of those high-rise buildings downtown."

Maxwell finished up the remnants of his breakfast. "That's a shame, Ma." He felt like he had been kicked in the stomach.

"I know," Marilyn agreed. "I've never cared much for women messing around with married men. On the other hand, I don't think Rose and Maxine should have let something like that interfere in their relationship."

Marilyn cleared the dishes from the table and placed them in the sink. Grabbing the coffee pot, she refilled each of their mugs. "Enough about them now, baby. How are things going with you?" Marilyn returned to her seat in front of Maxwell.

"I'm good, Ma. There's nothing major to report on my end."

Marilyn studied her son. She could see a hint of sadness in his eyes. "Whatever happened to that young lady you were interested in? I haven't heard you mention her in a while."

"Things didn't work out," Maxwell said flatly, hoping Marilyn would drop the subject.

"What happened? You were crazy about her. Did she cheat on you or something?" Marilyn pressed.

"No, it wasn't anything like that. I found out something major about her, and it was more than I wanted to deal with."

"What could have been that devastating? Did she have a criminal background or something? Was she hiding a bunch of kids you didn't know about?" Marilyn could tell Maxwell wanted to drop the subject, but she wasn't giving up that easily.

"I found out she has HIV," he stated firmly.

"Oh," Marilyn said. Her eyes widened at Maxwell's confession. She told you that? How did she get it?" Marilyn questioned.

"No, she didn't tell me. I found some medication at her house the day I cleaned your gutters. I found out the next morning what the medicine was for."

"Knowing you the way I do, I'm sure you confronted her. How did she say she got it?"

"She didn't say. I asked her why she didn't tell me, and she kept asking me to let her explain. At that point, I was done. I didn't want to hear anything else she had to say."

Marilyn held her breath. Her nerves threatened to overtake her. "Son, have you been tested?" she asked, silently praying he hadn't become infected as well.

"What? No, I didn't get tested. She and I never crossed that line. I'm a minister, Mama." Maxwell found himself becoming angry.

"Why didn't you give her a chance to explain then? From what you're telling me, she never put you at risk of getting the virus."

"She knew I had feelings for her. She should have told me about it, and given me the option whether to remain in her life or not," he shouted. "She took that option away from me by choosing to keep quiet about it."

Marilyn matched his tone. "First of all, you better stop yelling up in here. I know you're mad, but don't get crazy. You better remember where you are and who you're talking to. If this is any indication of how you talked to her, it's no wonder you and her no longer talk."

"Ma, I'm sorry, but you keep pressing and pressing. Why won't you let this go? Everybody seems to want to take her side. Nobody is considering what this has done to me."

"I don't think everybody is taking her side. Tell me something. What would you have done if the shoe was on the other foot? What if you were the one with the disease? Would you have told her?"

"That's not fair, Ma."

"Why isn't it fair? You said she knew you had feelings for her, but you never said you and her were a couple. Quite honestly, I can't promise you that if I was in that situation I would openly reveal it to people. That's a hard thing to divulge to people. You never know how people are going to react.

Marilyn walked around the table and put her arms around Maxwell. "Baby, the woman never put you at risk. That should count for something. I know you had feelings for her, and I can even understand your being upset. Baby, you owe it to her and you owe it to yourself to talk to her. You are not going to have peace until you do." Marilyn patted Maxwell on the chest. "Your heart won't let you. You're not that kind of person, baby."

He considered his mother's words. She was right about one thing for sure. He didn't have peace. In fact, he had been walking around feeling hollow inside. He turned to Maxine, thinking he would find solace in her, but as it turns out, she was probably living a lie also.

Chapter 41

Maxwell pulled his vehicle away from the curb and drove in the direction of the store. Without warning, he made an unplanned turn and pulled onto the expressway. Almost involuntarily, he maneuvered in and out of traffic. He drove like a man on a mission. Twenty minutes later, he pulled into the covered parking lot and retrieved a ticket from the attendant. Circling the parking lot, he found a suitable space and parked his vehicle.

Walking out to the street, he looked at the addresses on the building. He stopped in front of the building with 25 Wacker Drive etched into the stone. Adjusting his suit jacket, he walked into the building. There was a young Asian man stationed at the information desk. Maxwell walked over to him.

Seeing Maxwell approach the desk, the young man smiled. "Hello, sir. Welcome to 25 Wacker Drive. How can I help you?"

"Uh, hi. I'm looking for an attorney," Maxwell said.

"I'll be glad to help you with that, sir. What area of expertise do you need?"

"I'm sorry; I didn't make myself very clear. I'm looking for Attorney Maxine Miller."

"Yes, sir. Do you know her suite number?"

Maxwell shook his head. "No, I'm sorry I don't."

"That's not a problem. I can look it up in our directory." The young man keyed Maxine's name into the computer using the keyword, attorney. *No match found* appeared across the screen. "It's coming up no match found, sir. Are you certain you have to correct building?"

"There must be some kind of mistake," Maxwell retorted. "I have her business card." Maxwell searched his wallet.

"Let me try another approach. Due to security measures we're required to list all employees no matter their role in our database. If she works anywhere in this building, she will be in this database." Within seconds, the young man smiled. "Here she is. *Maxine Miller–Paralegal–Freeman, Reynolds and Associates.* Their office is located in suite number 1038. If you'll take the elevators to the left, they will take you to the tenth floor. You'll need to turn left off the elevator."

"Thank you," Maxwell said with a forced smile.

Maxwell followed the clerk's instructions. A short elevator ride later, he stood in front of Maxine's office suite. He hesitated to enter, but he had come too far to back out. As he approached the door, one of Maxine's coworkers noticed him.

"Hey, Maxwell," she said. Figuring he wouldn't remember her, she reminded him of their meeting at one of the restaurants he and Maxine had visited.

"Oh yeah, hey. How have you been?"

"I've been good. I don't have to ask how you've been. Judging by those beautiful flowers you sent Maxine this morning I would say you're doing pretty good."

Maxwell felt like he had been hit by a steamroller. Not wanting to cause a scene, he smiled and went along with the game. "Where is that lovely lady of mine?" he asked.

"The paralegal room is right through here. Her desk is over in the back corner."

"Thank you," Maxwell said. I can't wait to see the look on her face when she sees me."

A crystal vase filled with exotic flowers sat on the end of the desk in the corner. *That must be her desk*, he thought. Maxine was busy drafting a pleading and didn't see him approaching.

"Hello, Maxine," he said, startling her.

She looked as if she had seen a ghost. "Maxwell, hey. What are you doing here?"

"Since you surprised me with lunch at the store, I figured I'd return the favor. Can you go now, or do you need permission from the office manager?" Maxwell's tone was harsh.

"Maxine, are you finished drafting that pleading? Mr. Reynolds needs it in his office right away," Maxine's supervisor spoke freely. She didn't realize Maxine had a visitor until Maxwell turned around. "Who are you?" she asked bluntly.

Extending his hand, Maxwell smiled. "I'm Maxwell Lee, pleased to meet you."

"The pleasure is mine," the office manager replied blushing. "So you're the mystery man that's sending all these beautiful flowers and gifts."

"Apparently so," Maxwell replied, looking at Maxine with a tight-lipped grin.

"He came to take me to lunch." Maxine spoke up distracting the office manager from Maxwell's statement.

"Oh, I see," she said. "I need that pleading before you can go."

"Okay, I need to make a few minor adjustments, and I'll be done."

Satisfied with her answer, the office manager started to walk away. Stopping she turned to Maxwell. "I don't know where my manners are today, Maxwell. Would you like a cup of coffee?"

"I'd love a cup of coffee."

"Great. Follow me and I'll show you where it is." Turning

to Maxine she said, "He'll be in the client waiting area when you're done."

Maxine entered the waiting room ten minutes later. Looking at Maxwell, she asked, "Are you ready to go?"

"Of course, I am. Lead the way."

Maxine's legs felt weak. There was no way she could talk her way out of a confrontation with Maxwell. With each step she took, her knees wobbled more and more.

Once they were safe outside the building, Maxwell grabbed her by her elbow and escorted her down the street. "I don't know which lie I should address first," he stated furiously. "I knew something wasn't right about you from the moment you walked into my store. It's not enough that you lied to my face constantly, you even went as far as to have your married boyfriend to send you flowers in my name." Maxwell's tone elevated. "Oh, yeah, by the way, your mother had a great time with her husband in Europe for the past month."

"How do you know where my mother was?" she shot back. Angry or not, he was not going to intimidate her.

"She ran into my mother at a restaurant and filled her in on all the glorious details of her gold digging daughter who loves to indulge in forbidden fruit. What was I, your front man? Is that why we always had to go to places that your coworkers magically appeared? What are you doing? Screwing your boss?"

"How dare you talk to me like that? You want to sit up and act like you're all that. If you weren't so busy seeking perfection, I wouldn't have been able to scoop you up so easily. You used me just as much as I used you." Pointing her finger in his face, she snarled, "You self-righteous pig. Before you step up trying to check me, you better check yourself. A gold-digger I may be, but I'm real with mine. And, baby, please know, you could never afford me. Get a grip and get a life." Maxine threw her hair over her shoulder and walked away leaving Maxwell alone on the sidewalk. Knowing her coworkers would be suspicious if she returned too quickly, she spent the extra time shopping. When she returned with the bags she would simply smile and say they were from Maxwell.

Chapter 42

"Wake up, sleepy head. You have a busy day ahead of you." Lydia kissed Lina on the forehead, awakening her from her slumber. "Are you trying to sleep all day?"

"Ma, leave me alone," Lina fussed. "I'm sleepy."

"Girl, please. Stop acting like a baby and get up." Laughing, Lydia snatched the covers off of Lina. "I cooked your favorite breakfast. Can't you smell it?"

Lina inhaled deeply, allowing the aroma from the kitchen to sink in. "Mmm, is that bacon I smell?"

"Yes, now get up." Lydia left Lina sitting up on the bed and returned to the kitchen to check on her meal.

Lina freshened up and joined her mother in the kitchen. Lydia was standing by the sink, washing the pots she'd used for breakfast. Lina stood and watched her mother swaying to the music playing on the radio. Tiptoeing, Lina walked up and embraced her mother from behind.

Lydia stood stiff as a board. "Girl, you scared me with your silly self," she shrieked, returning Lina's embrace.

"Where's daddy?" Lina asked, looking around the kitchen. He's obviously not in here, and I didn't see him in the living room."

"He had to run a few errands this morning. He'll be back after a while."

"What about breakfast?" Lina asked, pouring herself a cup of coffee.

"He's already eaten. You know that man likes to get up early and start his day with breakfast. After forty years of marriage I'm still getting up and getting it done." Lydia took a seat at the table. "Come on over here. I haven't eaten. I wanted to wait and eat with my baby."

Lina smiled and complied. "Everything looks good, Mama," Lina said as she placed a few slices of bacon, a spoonful of eggs and a few spoons of grits on her plate.

"Thank you, baby, I hope you'll enjoy it."

"Uh huh," Lina hummed, nodding her head with a mouthful of food.

Lydia rose and went to the oven. Removing hot, buttered biscuits, she placed two on Lina's plate and repeated the same for herself.

Lina picked up her coffee and took a sip. "I need to hurry up so I can go and see my baby today. I am so in love with that little boy." She smiled at the thought of her nephew. "I want to get a few more pictures of him."

"My poor grandson doesn't stand a chance with his Auntie Lina and that camera. With all that flashing he sees, it's a wonder he's not blind."

"Ooh, Mama, you know I can't make him blind from my camera. Besides, he's so cute, the camera loves him. I told Zarion I would spend the night tonight so that they can get some sleep. He's wearing them out."

"I imagine he is." Lydia thought back to the days when her children were newborns. Her husband worked long hours so she was left doing the childcare. Middle of the night feedings, diaper changes, and colicky babies were common.

"Anyway, I'll clean the kitchen since you cooked. When I get done, I'm gonna head on over there." Transportation for Lina wasn't an issue because her parents kept the old Toyota Camry she drove when she was in college. It wasn't the cutest vehicle on the road, but it got her from point A to point B. Besides, she didn't have anyone she was trying to impress.

"I spoke with Zarion earlier this morning and she said she had to take Daniel for his two-week check-up today. You should probably check with her before you go all the way over there."

"That's right," Lina said, snapping her fingers. "I forget all about his appointment. In that case, I'll go and take some random photos to add to my portfolio. It'll be nice to have some pictures of different scenery."

"Actually, I was hoping you and I could spend the day together," Lydia interrupted. "We could have a girl's day out and catch up."

Lina looked at her mother somewhat confused. She hadn't had a day out alone with her mother since she graduated college. "Okay, we can do that," she agreed.

Rising from the table, Lydia said, "You go ahead and get dressed and meet me back in here so we can go. We'll probably go to the mall or something."

"That sounds good, Mama." Lina hurried to her bedroom to prepare for the day. If her mother was offering her a trip to the mall, she was not going to turn it down.

Lydia sat on the couch watching television while she waited for Lina. A half hour later, Lina joined her in the living room.

"I'm ready," she announced. "Don't I look cute?"

Turning to assess her daughter's outfit, Lydia smiled. "Yes, you do, baby."

She wore black slacks and a vibrant, purple, off-the-shoulder top. Her hair was pulled back with a striped purple and black headband. Solid black, hoop earrings, and a silver necklace with a black onyx pendant rounded out her accessories. A pair of pleated, black flats completed her outfit.

Lina handed her mother her purse from the end table and followed her to the car. Lydia cautiously backed out of the driveway, and carefully drove off. A series of car accidents and near misses caused her to be more cautious when she drove. "This isn't so bad, is it?" she asked, glancing over at Lina.

"You mean other than the fact that we just got passed by a man on a walker?" Lina laughed at her own joke. "I'm just playing, this is fine."

Lydia hit at her like she was swatting a fly. "Very funny," she said shaking her head from side to side in mock sarcasm. "Child, you are just like your old daddy, always thinking you're a comedian."

Making a left turn, Lydia maneuvered her car onto the expressway. "Since I have you here, I do want to talk to you. You know, find out what's going on in your life these days."

"Nothing much," Lina replied quickly. She wasn't in the mood for another one of her mother's lectures.

Lydia continued, pretending not to notice Lina's snappy response. "A few months ago you called and told me about a guy you had met and became good friends with. You have been home for two weeks now, and I haven't heard you mention him once. I haven't even seen you on the phone talking to anyone other than Cheri. What's up with that?"

Lina laughed inwardly at her mother's attempt to sound cool at the end of her question. "Nothing is up with that, as you say, Mama. You haven't heard me mention him because there is nothing to mention. We're not friends anymore."

In a way, Lydia was surprised, but then again she wasn't. She could pretty much guess what happened without Lina telling her. Not being the one to assume normally, she decided to wait for Lina to fill her in on the details.

"What happened?" Lydia asked earnestly.

"Nothing, Mama," Lina replied.

"Tell that to somebody that doesn't know you. You can skirt around it all you want, but a mother knows her child. Now, tell me what's going on in Chicago."

Lina considered her mother's words. She knew she didn't have anything to lose by letting her mother know what happened between her and Maxwell. In reality, her mother could offer her some much needed support.

"A couple of months ago I had a bad cold. A very bad cold, I thought it was the flu; it was so bad. Cheri was out of town for her job, so she asked Maxwell to come over to check on me. He came by, fixed me something to eat, and gave me some cold medicine. While he was there, he went to use my bathroom and saw my medicine on the sink." She gave her mother a familiar glance. "You know the rest."

Tapping Lina on the leg, Lydia offered her support. "Baby, I'm sorry you had to go through that. It may not seem that way now, but things will get better. God is going to send you the man that will accept you for who you are. He will love you in spite of your condition. Hold on, and be encouraged."

"I'm good, Mama, I really am. One thing you taught me is no matter how bad things seem initially, in time it will pass."

Lydia was proud of the woman her youngest daughter had become. She realized she wouldn't always be there to protect Lina from hurtful things. She was glad she and her husband had given their children a solid foundation. They taught them to always pray, whether things were going good or bad. From childhood, they reassured them that they would always have the love and support of their parents.

Upon arriving at the mall, Lydia found a park close to the mall entrance. Lina jumped out and ran around to the driver's door. "Come on, Mama, let's burn up that credit card.

Chapter 43

"Why does this stuff keep happening to me?" Maxwell questioned. Anger and frustration left him feeling numb. It seemed like every time he wanted to move forward in a relationship, something major happened, derailing him. In some ways, he blamed himself for the way things turned out between him and Maxine. He knew from the beginning she was not a good mate for him. He chose to ignore all the warning signs.

As much as he hated to admit it, Maxine was right. He had used her to get over Lina. She was available, and he thought she was convenient. She occupied the space he wanted filled by a female companion. He used their childhood friendship as a way to justify spending time with her. In the back of his mind, he secretly wanted a way out. The way Maxine behaved the one time she visited his church made it virtually impossible for her to come back, especially as his wife.

Maxine's over the top personality and expensive lifestyle would quickly alienate the women of the congregation. If he was going to be pastor he had to have the perfect wife, anything less would hurt his ministry. So far, he kept pulling weeds. The more he thought about his confrontation with Maxine, the more upset he became.

Maxwell didn't feel like going home, because home would be a constant reminder of his poor choices in women. He wasn't in the right frame of mind to go to work. His staff would easily pick up on his lack of focus. Going to his mother's house was completely out of the question. Exhausted, he went to the only place that he would be able to find peace.

Pulling into the church parking lot, Maxwell parked close to the building. The janitorial staff worked on Saturday and Tuesday, therefore he knew he would be alone. Once he was secure inside, he made his way to the sanctuary. He approached the altar. With tears in his eyes, he dropped to his knees and prayed. He prayed like a child crying out to his father. He asked the Lord to forgive him and to heal his heart. He sought the Lord for direction and peace.

Maxwell knew in his heart he hadn't done all he should in the ministry. He had gotten so caught up in finding a wife that he had left his first love. He knew he could no longer blame Lina and Maxine for his heartache. He lost his focus and became more concerned about his desires rather than the Lord's will for his life.

"I'm sorry, Lord. Please forgive me. I'll do better, I'll be better, just please, help me, Heavenly Father."

When he finished praying, he took a seat on the pew at the front of the church. The sound of footsteps broke through the silence of the building. "How are you doing, son?" Pastor James asked, as he approached Maxwell."

"I'm sorry, Pastor. I didn't know you were here. I would have spoken to you had I known."

"It's all right. I just got here. I like to come by the church sometimes during the week. I saw your vehicle parked outside." Pastor James sat on the pew next to Maxwell. "What's troubling you so?"

"I don't know, Pastor. I've messed up a lot of things. Now, more than ever, I need God to step in and fix them."

Pastor James displayed the compassion of a father. "Son, you and I both know you can't use God like a genie in a bottle. He doesn't just pop up and fix the messes we make. He requires action on our part as well."

"I know. But to be quite honest with you, I don't know how to fix it. I don't even know where to start."

"What is it you're not telling me? I can't help you if continue to hold back. I'm not a mind reader."

Maxwell trusted Pastor James and found him easy to talk to. He told him he was having a hard time dealing with Lina's positive HIV status and Maxine's deception. He shared with him the events of the day, including the things he learned concerning Maxine. He gave him a detailed recount of his confrontation with Maxine and the anger it brought him. "Pastor, sometimes I wonder if God is even still with me," Maxwell confessed.

"I see," is all Pastor James said, allowing Maxwell to express his feelings uninterrupted. When Maxwell grew quiet, Pastor James asked him politely, "Are you ready for me to speak now, son?"

"Sure, go ahead," Maxwell replied

"Son, do you recall a little while back when I called you after church?"

Maxwell nodded his head, "Yes."

"If you recall that conversation, then you recall me telling you to wait on the Lord. You were so excited and caught up in the moment that you didn't heed my words. I didn't know why I felt led to tell you that. Sometimes blessings come in forms we don't expect." Pastor James shook his head. "I remember hearing you say, any way God sees fit to bless you, you'll be satisfied."

"One thing about the Lord, son, He won't put more on us than we can bear. Some things seem unbearable when we initially face them. Oh, but if we hold on, we soon realize we can handle more than we thought we could." Pastor James spoke with a calm boldness. "You know there's a saying that goes, 'you can't see the forest for the trees'. That saying simply means sometimes we miss out on what's right in front of us because we're seeking more."

"Son, there are some things you've done that you have to make right. Seek the Lord, He'll give you direction. Now, you must remember when the Lord leads you and gives you instruction you have to obey." Pastor James pulled himself to a standing position. "I wouldn't be right if I didn't tell you, the peace you seek won't come until you make things right. I love you, son." Pastor James walked away, leaving Maxwell alone with his thoughts.

Without question, his mind drifted to Lina. He knew in his heart he had treated her unfairly. He didn't consider her feelings or her reputation when he confronted her on the church parking lot. He was selfish and didn't stop to think about what life was like for her. He knew he needed to seek her forgiveness, but he didn't know how he would do it. He hadn't seen her in months and he was sure Cheri wouldn't give him her contact information. All he could do was hope for a chance meeting like the ones they had in the beginning.

Maxwell left the church with a goal in mind. He had to make things right.

Chapter 44

"It's about time you got back," Cheri yelled through the phone. "I missed you. Three and a half weeks is way too long for you to be gone."

"I missed you too, Cheri, with your crazy self." Lina sat her suitcase on the bed and started unpacking. She had opted for an evening flight so that she didn't have to rush to the airport. She hated leaving her family, but she knew she had to get back. She was building a life she was proud of in Chicago. "I enjoyed myself, but I have to admit, after a while I started missing my apartment. There's nothing like having your own space."

"I hear you," Cheri agreed. "How's everybody doing? How was the baby when you left?"

Lina pulled her lips into a big, toothy smile. "Girl, he is perfect. I know I took hundreds of pictures of him. I didn't know you could love someone else's child that much. You'll never guess the best part."

"What was that?" Cheri asked with excitement.

"Zarion and her husband asked me to be Daniel's God-mother."

"What did you say?" Cheri inquired.

"Are you serious right now? You know I said, yes. I was so proud and honored that they would ask me. Oh, and please believe I am taking my auntie slash God-mother duties seriously."

"I hear you, girl. I'm happy for you, Lina."

"Thank you. Everyone else is doing well too. My mom took

me on a shopping spree while I was there. You're gonna have to come over and see all the stuff I got." Lina moved into the living room and took a seat on the couch. "So, tell me what's been going on?"

"You mean other than all the stuff I told you during our phone conversations? Nothing, really." Cheri paused. "I almost forgot. Pastor James asked about you. He told me to tell you he misses seeing you at the church, and that he and his wife are praying for you."

"That's nice to know," Lina replied nonchalantly.

"What's up with that?" Cheri asked defensively.

"I'm sorry; I guess I associate everything about that church with Maxwell. I know I shouldn't do that. I must not be over it," she admitted.

"I understand. Some things take longer to get over than others. Speaking of Maxwell, there's something different about him. I can't put my finger on it, but it's something."

"I don't mean any harm, but I don't want to talk about him. I'm sure you understand."

"Yeah, I understand," Cheri agreed.

Lina completed her call with Cheri. After putting away her things, she took a bath and turned in for the evening.

Chapter 45

Charles Davenport flipped through the mock-up. As the Executive Editor of *About Us* magazine, it was his job to personally check the entire layout. He took special notice of the photos in the upcoming issue. As with other issues, pictures by Lina Fairweather stood out to him. He buzzed his secretary.

"Elizabeth, please get Lina Fairweather on the phone. Ask her if she can meet with me this afternoon to discuss her work."

"Yes, Mr. Davenport," she replied. Elizabeth searched through her contacts on the computer for Lina's phone number.

Lina sat on the couch, munching on caramel popcorn as she watched reruns of her favorite gospel singing competition. She was amazed by the talent displayed by regular people, that had previously been unknown by most. Watching others achieve their dreams both uplifted and encouraged her.

Her phone rang loudly, distracting her. Since her cell phone served as both her business line as well as her personal line she was always careful to answer professionally on numbers she didn't recognize. Using the remote control, she muted the television.

"Lina Fairweather speaking. How may I help you?"

"Hello, Miss Fairweather. My name is Elizabeth Lawrence with *About Us* magazine. I'm calling on behalf of the Executive Editor, Mr. Charles Davenport. Mr. Davenport has requested a meeting with you this afternoon, if you are available."

Lina was stunned at the request. Why would the Executive Editor want to meet with her? She usually only dealt with the

Photo Editor. "Yes, I'm available. What time does he want me to be there?" she asked, trying not to sound too eager.

"He has openings at one o'clock and also three o'clock. Which time would be most convenient for you, Miss Fairweather?"

"One o'clock is fine," Lina replied.

"Okay, great. I'll let Mr. Davenport know to expect you. Your meeting will be held at our corporate office downtown, 814 South Wacker Drive, Suite 328C."

"I'll be there, thank you." Lina placed her cell phone on the small table next to the couch. She only had a couple of hours to prepare for the meeting. She needed to re-organize her portfolio, and select the perfect outfit. *What could Mr. Davenport possibly want to meet with me about?* she wondered.

****

Lina arrived fifteen minutes early for her appointment. With her portfolio tucked neatly under her arm, she approached the executive suite. Large, smoked gray doors with chrome handles offered an opening to the spacious office. A glass desk, trimmed in white, sat a few feet away from the entrance. Black leather chairs were placed in an L shape in the corner of the room. A round glass coffee table sat in front of the chairs. As she approached the reception desk, she was greeted with a warm smile. Returning the smile with one of her own, Lina introduced herself.

"Hi, I'm Lina Fairweather. I have a one o'clock appointment with Mr. Davenport."

"Hello, Miss Fairweather. I'm Elizabeth. We spoke on the phone. Mr. Davenport is currently on a conference call. He should be finishing up any moment now. I'll take your coat for you." Elizabeth directed Lina to the chairs in the reception area. "If you would, please have a seat and I will let him know you have arrived. Would you like something to drink while you wait?"

"No, thank you, I'm fine." Lina replied, before walking over to the small waiting area. Previous issues of *About Us* were neatly displayed on the small coffee table. She picked up the copy on top and thumbed through the pages. She felt butterflies in her stomach when she saw several of her pictures placed throughout the magazine.

"Miss Fairweather, Mr. Davenport will see you now. Please, go right in," Elizabeth announced pointing her in the direction of Charles' office.

Lina gathered her belongings and walked nervously into Charles Davenport's office. A gold nameplate hung on the door with Charles Davenport Executive Editor embossed on it.

Charles stood and walked around the desk to greet her. He smiled broadly, as he shook her hand. "Miss Fairweather, thanks for meeting with me on such short notice." He offered her a seat in front of his shiny, solid black desk before returning to his seat behind the desk.

"This isn't the way I normally do business, but there is a bit of urgency in my request."

Lina sat quietly as Charles explained to her the reason for their sudden meeting.

Charles leaned back in the large black leather chair as he spoke. "Miss Fairweather, I review every issue of *About Us* Magazine before it is sent to print. For several months now, I have admired the photos you have submitted for publication. I met with my photo editor and found out you're a freelance photographer.

I asked you here today because I would like to offer you a full time position as a staff photographer. I know you are probably wondering why I'm the one offering you this position as opposed to the Photo Editor. You see, Miss Fairweather, this is a special position. The person I am looking for will be placed on exclusive assignments. This position requires occasional travel, and at times odd hours. Basically, whatever it takes to get the job done will be required."

Removing a manila folder from his desk drawer Charles slid it over to Lina. "Please take a look."

Lina picked the folder up from the desk and scanned its contents. She took a deep breath, trying to calm her nerves when she saw typed in bold print $65,000.00 annual salary. Underneath the salary, fringe benefits were listed. Full medical and dental benefits without restrictions for pre-existing conditions, paid travel, and vacations, paid sick leave, short and long term disability benefits and a sizable retirement plan, rounded off the list of benefits. On the second page, there was a detailed outline of job requirements and functions. The contract included a clause stating Lina would be allowed to continue her freelance photography, as long as her subjects didn't conflict with her work for the magazine. Everything appeared to be planned out and in order. Finding her voice, she looked at Charles and said, "This is a very generous offer. I appreciate you considering me. How soon do you need an answer?"

"I need an answer before the end of the week. I have a very important assignment coming up soon, and I need to have everyone in place at least two weeks before the event. I need someone who can start work as soon as possible. Feel free to take the papers home and review them and get back with me on or before Friday."

Lina was ready to jump up and down and scream, yes, but she didn't want to seem overly eager. She didn't want Mr. Davenport to think he had made a poor choice. Her praise party was going to have to wait until she was in her car. "Thank you,

Mr. Davenport. I'll look it over, and get back with you as soon as possible."

Charles stood and escorted her to the door. "Miss Fairweather, I must ask you to please keep the details of your offer confidential. As I mentioned earlier, this is a special position with special benefits."

"Yes sir, Mr. Davenport I understand." Lina shook his hand again before leaving his office.

Once she was secure in her car, Lina shouted praises to God. "Thank you, Lord. Lord, I love you. Thank you, Jesus." She could hardly wait to get home to call her parents and Cheri. Lina drove home laughing and singing. Things in her life were looking up more than ever. She knew she only had the Lord to thank. Truly God had smiled on her.

Upon arriving home, Lina laid the folder containing her job offer on the table. She pulled out the paper and called her parents right away. She read the offer to them word for word. She didn't want to take a chance on leaving anything out. Lina recalled Mr. Davenport asking her to keep the offer confidential, but she gladly excluded her parents from the do not tell list. Mr. and Mrs. Fairweather shared their daughter's enthusiasm. They expressed their pride in her and encouraged her to accept the offer.

Lina found it extremely difficult holding off on her decision to accept the job offer. She decided to call Mr. Davenport before he was scheduled to leave for the day. She informed Elizabeth of her desire to speak with him. After a brief hold, he picked up on the line.

"Miss Fairweather, I didn't expect to hear from you so soon. I hope you have good news for me."

"I do, Mr. Davenport," she replied, "I have thought it over, and I've decided to accept your offer."

"That's great," he exclaimed. "Now that you have accepted the offer, I can fill you in on the details of your first assignment. I was given the distinct honor of interviewing the First family at their home in Washington DC. You will be accompanying me as the photographer."

Lina could not believe what she was hearing. She could no longer mask her excitement. "Are you serious, you want me to photograph the president and his family? Oh my God, I can't believe this."

Charles laughed as he listened to Lina express her gratitude. His reaction was the same as hers when he received the call from the office of the President's Press Secretary. "Yes, Miss Fairweather, I am very serious. How soon can you start?"

"Right away, sir. I can start right away," she exclaimed.

"Good, I need you to come in tomorrow morning at eight o'clock so that we can take care of the necessary paperwork and discuss your assignment."

"Yes, sir, I'll be there." Lina hung up the phone and jumped around her apartment until she made herself exhausted. She would have to fill Cheri in on the details later. God had blessed her abundantly.

Chapter 46

Maxwell turned over and pounded the pillow with his fist. Sleep escaped him. His mind was constantly racing. It seemed as if every word he had spoken concerning Lina, and everything thing they had experienced together, played in his mind like a never-ending movie. Gripping the pillow with both hands, he squeezed as tightly as he could, hoping to ease the mounting tension that settled in his neck and shoulders.

Who was he fooling? He knew he wouldn't be able to go another day without talking to her. He didn't think it would be a good idea to show up at her apartment unannounced. Reaching her on the phone didn't appear promising. This was something that needed to be done in person. After weeks of begging and pleading, he had finally convinced Cheri to help him locate Lina so that he could make things right.

"I have to get this done, today," he declared aloud. Forcing himself out of bed, he prepared for the day. Maxwell recalled the expression on Lina's face when she saw him dressed casually. Knowing he would need all the help he could get, he opted for a pair of jeans and a solid black shirt.

He prayed earnestly as he traveled downtown. He didn't know what to expect upon seeing Lina, so he asked God to soften her heart. He prayed she would accept his apology and see the change in him. Since his conversation with Pastor James, Maxwell had chosen to educate himself on the illness that plagued Lina's body. He joined several internet message boards where he communicated with others living with HIV.

He was impressed by their candidness as they described what life was like for them. They shared stories of ill treatment they received from people after their illness was revealed. Reading their stories gave him a chance to see the fragileness of their hearts. Most of them simply wanted to live their lives without ridicule.

Maxwell parked a couple of blocks away from Lina's office building. He filled the parking meter with several quarters. He didn't know how long his meeting with Lina would take, and he didn't want to risk receiving a ticket or even worse, getting towed. He looked at the time and figured Lina would be exiting the building soon. The short walk gave him the chance to ponder what he would say to her.

Lina walked out of the building with several of her coworkers. She laughed as they spoke about the events of the day. Lina found it easy to make friends after joining the staff at About Us Magazine. She and her coworkers often went out to lunch together, and sometimes met up for dinner. Soon they dispersed in different directions leaving her alone. Her car was in the repair shop, causing her to use public transportation. She stood patiently at the CTA bus stop and waited for her bus to arrive.

Drawing in a deep breath, Maxwell called out to her. "Lina."

Startled by the familiar voice, she rolled her eyes and turned slowly. "Yes," she answered. As much as she hated to admit it, the sound of Maxwell's voice still had an effect on her.

"How are you?" Seeing Lina after so much time stirred up feelings in Maxwell he was sure had ceased.

"I'm fine." She wanted to express anger but Maxwell's eyes held a sincerity that she couldn't deny.

"That's good. I'm glad to hear that." He looked down at the ground and then back up at Lina. I hope you don't mind me approaching you like this, but I really need to talk to you. I didn't know any other way to get to you. It wouldn't have been appropriate for me to come to your apartment uninvited. Is there any way we could go somewhere and talk? I promise I won't hold you long.

Lina looked at her watch and then down the street. Her bus was nowhere in sight. "Sure, why not," she agreed. Lina adjusted the laptop bag on her shoulder.

"Here, let me take that for you."

Maxwell removed the bag from Lina's shoulder and placed it on his own before she could protest. Although she wanted to refuse the offer, the relief she felt wouldn't allow her to. The cool, evening air caused Lina to shiver. The autumn weather was unpredictable. She wore a jacket, but it was proving to be unsatisfactory.

Maxwell noticed her shivering. He offered to go to a restaurant where they could talk and warm up, but Lina refused.

"My vehicle is parked a couple of blocks from here. If you don't mind, I'd be glad to take you home. That way we can talk openly, and you won't have to ride the bus. You know my seats are much softer than the seats on the CTA," Maxwell joked. He was surprised when he saw a smile crease Lina's lips.

Lina knew the pending conversation between her and Maxwell would be as beneficial to her as it would him. Without debate, she agreed to have him take her home. They walked to the truck in awkward silence. She trusted him to be kind to her in his words. She reasoned within, he wouldn't go through all the trouble that he had in order to start another fight.

Arriving at Maxwell's vehicle, he opened the door and stepped aside for Lina to enter. Closing her door, he walked around to the driver's side and slid under the steering wheel. Turning to look at her, he held her gaze. "Lina, I'm sorry. The way I treated you and spoke to you that day at the church was wrong. You never deserved to be talked to that way. On that day, I spoke out of ignorance. I looked at the situation with blinders on. I reacted without thinking."

Maxwell sat back and rested his head on the back of the seat. "I felt like something precious had been taken away from me, and I didn't know how to handle it." Maxwell took a long pause before confessing, "I had fallen in love with you, Lina. I never told you because I didn't want to push you away. You always seemed to pull back from me when I pressed forward, so I decided to go at the pace that I thought was comfortable for you."

Lina looked at Maxwell in disbelief. She struggled with her own feelings. Part of her wanted to tell him, she shared his feelings. The other part of her wanted to nurse the wounds he had inflicted on her heart. Tears flowed easily from her eyes.

Finding her voice, she confessed. "I fell in love with you too, Maxwell. The problem was I knew my situation. I wasn't ready to reveal it to you because I felt the moment I did, you would run away. In order to keep you in my life, I kept quiet, and I held you at arm's length. I figured if I didn't allow the relationship to cross from friends to being a couple, I could have the pleasure of your company without facing the reality of my illness. I knew you would look at me differently, and I was right, Maxwell. I was right. You were so mean to me. Your words were cruel."

Maxwell reached in the console and handed Lina a handkerchief. "Lina, I could spend the rest of my life telling you how sorry I am. It may make a difference and it may not. God knows I never meant to hurt you." His voice broke as he spoke.

"And I never wanted to hurt you," Lina retorted. "I tried so hard to keep this from happening."

Closing his eyes, Maxwell fought back tears of his own. His heart yearned to be loved by Lina. He thought about Victoria and Jeremy's unconditional love. He wondered what things would be like if he was the one infected and not Lina. Would she be willing to be in his life, or would she have turned her back on him?

Turning to her, he grabbed her hand. "Lina, I'm not the man I used to be. I know this illness is big, but our God is so much bigger. When I walked away from you, my life seemed to take a downward spiral. It wasn't until I truly sought the Lord that I realized you were the missing piece to my puzzle. If you'll have me, I want to be the man in your life. I want to endow you with the unconditional love that God gives us."

"But my disease, Maxwell." Shaking her head, she continued, "It's not going anywhere. Yes, I know God is able to heal me, but I also have accepted the fact that He may not. I will never give birth to children of my own. I'll never be able to live like someone without the illness. I'll have good days, and I'll have some horrible days. I can't ask you to take that journey with me. It wouldn't be fair to you."

"Sweetheart, I've considered it all, and I'm willing to be everything you need. I love you, Lina, and nothing is going to change that. Not even your illness. I now realize what it means in the Bible where it says, God will not put more on us than we can bear. It's because when things seems unbearable and we become weak, God holds us up and renews our strength." Wiping the tears from Lina's eyes, Maxwell kissed her lips and said, "My strength has been renewed, now let me carry you."

~The End~

About the Author

LaCricia A`ngelle is a licensed Evangelist, writer, and publisher. A native of Chicago, she currently resides in Tennessee with her husband and children. This is her second novel.

To arrange signings, book events, or speaking engagements or to send comments to the author please email her at:
author@lacriciaangelle.com or
authorlacricia@ymail.com.

Visit LaCricia A`ngelle online at:

www.lacriciaangelle.com or
www.facebook.com/lacriciaangelle

Your Personal Invitation

Behold, I stand at the door and knock. If anyone hears My voice and opens the door, I will come in to him and dine with him, and he with Me.
Romans 3:20 NKJV

As we go through life we often seek ways to fill void areas in our hearts. Whatever you may be seeking, you can find it in a personal relationship with Jesus Christ.

If you believe God is knocking on the door of your heart, this is your opportunity to welcome Him into your life.

If you have never accepted Jesus Christ as your personal Lord, and Savior, I extend to you this invitation.

CPSIA information can be obtained
at www.ICGtesting.com
Printed in the USA
FSOW01n1502250517
34397FS